White Feather

By
Nancy McIntosh Pafford

I hope you enjoy White Feather's story is

Nancy M Pafford

Catch the Spirit of Appalachia, Inc.
Western North Carolina

FIRST PRINTING 2004
SECOND PRINTING 2005
THIRD PRINTING 2006
FOURTH PRINTING 2007

Note to the Reader: The story of White Feather and
other characters are fictional; however, the events in
the story are based on factual research accounts of
the history of the Cherokee people.

Edited by Amy Ammons Garza
Cover Illustration by Doreyl Ammons Cain

Published by
SAN NO. 8 5 1 – 0 8 8 1
Catch the Spirit of Appalachia, Inc.
29 Regal Avenue, Sylva, NC 28779
Phone: 828-631-4587

Library of Congress Control Number: 2004100793

ISBN 0-9753023-0-2

Dedicated to the Cherokee People
Past   Present   Future

CONTENTS

CONTENTS

Prologue

The picture in the magazine I held in my hands leaped out at me, my gaze riveting to the Indian woman. She rode a bay horse, determination stamped on her face. Two small children on a pony followed close behind.

For a moment I stared, then glanced at the title below the picture. "Journey Home," it read. Again, I gazed at the face of the young woman wearing a white feather in her hair. I could feel the pull of her energy, until it seemed she was speaking to me.

"Write my story," her face begged.

"I'm not a writer," I replied silently.

"Write my story," came the words.

For a long time I sat motionless, finally naming the woman "White Feather."

"She's going home," I mouthed. "Home!"

Slowly the essence of what I imagined could have happened in the lives of White Feather and her Cherokee people came into my mind. The story took shape, and still I hesitated.

"I want to tell White Feather's story, but I don't have time," I thought. "I teach school...I'm so busy."

Still, the history of the Cherokee people had always fascinated me. Through the years I had read extensively about their culture and traditions, but I knew I would need even more information, more history, if I were to write a book.

Again, I glanced at the picture of White Feather. The plea in her eyes seemed to grow more intense. I could feel my excuses melting away, and I knew I had to tell her story.

But how should I begin?

"I must go back in time, back to the 1800s when it all began...back to the time the white government forced the Cherokee people living in the East to move to the West," I thought. Writing her story would require dedicated time.

"I will make time!" I suddenly declared.

And there, in that moment in time, my life changed. I picked up pen and writing pad, and nodding to White Feather, my thoughts slipped from my mind through my heart into my hand onto the paper.

On June 6, 1993, White Feather came over the mountains and rode the wind alongside me, giving me a story to tell,,,her story.

Thank You

Amy Ammons Garza

My editor   My teacher   My friend

And to....
    Zellna Shaw, who has been the wind beneath my sails; Tim, my son, for his support; Vickie; the Cherokee Historical Association (especially Lane and Alan); Bo Taylor in the Archives Department of the Museum of the Cherokee Indian; the Oconaluftee Indian Village; friends who encouraged me; and the many Cherokee people I have interviewed while writing this book. And my thanks goes to Doreyl Ammons Cain, who listened to my heart and captured the image of White Feather in her illustration.

White Feather

By Nancy McIntosh Pafford

CHAPTER ONE

Home—Spring, 1837

White Feather basked in the glory of a new day. The young Cherokee woman sighed deeply and wrapped her arms around her body as a smile crossed her face. She stood on the porch of her log cabin and gazed at the panoramic view of the majestic hazy blue-green mountains surrounding her home. Contentedly, she listened.

The breeze brought the flutter of leaves, bird songs floated from the nearby trees, and the water danced gently over the rocks in the river...all were like melodic music falling on White Feather's ears. She stood perfectly still, looking at the mountains, allowing the music to move her senses. Her gaze embraced the distant misty mountains.

The sights and sounds around her home never failed to warm White Feather's heart. Her 20 years had been spent in this peaceful valley of the Cherokee Indian land. Now White Feather had no desire to be anywhere other than here.

Shifting her weight, White Feather turned slowly and looked back through the open doorway of the log cabin to the corner of the room where Little Fawn lay sleeping on her bed. White Feather gazed at her first-born; remembering the continuous joy the child had brought to her since the infant's birth two springs ago.

"And soon," White Feather thought, patting her swollen belly, "another child will come to bring more happiness to us." She smiled. White Feather's heart leapt at the thought that the serene beauty of the land of their Cherokee people would surround her heirs.

Turning back to face the mountains, the woman walked slowly to the edge of the porch. She squinted her eyes against the bright light of the early morning sun, and raised her hand above her eyes to shade them. The sun, now quickly appearing from behind the mountains, cast its rays across the porch, bathing White Feather's body in its warmth. Her gaze quickly darted beyond the colorful wild flowers growing in the yard toward the river in search of her husband, Running Deer. The Cherokee man stood busy at work near the river.

Running Deer had been out of bed long before sunrise, quickly moving around outside the cabin tending to chores on the farm. Earlier he had paused briefly to share the morning meal with White Feather; now he had resumed his work, kneeling to pull the few scattered weeds out of the garden that would soon provide food for his family.

His turbaned head bent low scanning the ground, Running Deer continued his search; his body moving quickly, anxious to complete the task so he could go into the woods and hunt for a rabbit or squirrel. White Feather had been asking him for days to bring home fresh meat so she could cook the stew the family enjoyed. Running Deer did not choose to leave

White Feather alone for a long period of time because the baby would be jumping down soon. But he would please his wife today, he had promised himself, and would go search for game.

White Feather watched Running Deer's strong, muscular body as he moved along the garden rows. He paused occasionally to lean down and quickly pull the unwanted weeds and cast them aside.

She remembered the first time she had seen Running Deer. Today, as then, she thought of him as the most handsome man she had ever seen. His tall frame was lean with wide strong shoulders. Dark eyes offset his long raven hair that moved with the wind like the deer.

"Running Deer is a good husband," she thought. "He is a caring father to Little Fawn."

White Feather bent slowly and lifted the wooden bucket that Running Deer had washed in the river and left on the top step for her earlier in the morning. She must hurry to the barn now, she thought, knowing the family's cow would be waiting.

She walked down the cabin's stone steps slowly, taking care not to slip and fall. She felt clumsy; her body had grown large with the unborn child.

Stepping into the yard, she stopped and looked again at Running Deer. Pausing from his work, he glimpsed her movement. A broad smile crossed his face.

White Feather's heart responded. She returned his smile and continued walking the short distance to the barn and the waiting cow.

She entered, picked up the low milking stool and placed it close to the cow's side. Sighing, she sat on it and put the milk pail under the cow. As she began her chore, White Feather's thoughts wandered back to her recent visit in the nearby village of her people; her thoughts returning to the talk she and Running Deer had heard from their friends.

The talk had been disturbing. White Feather had not been able to erase it from her mind during the past few days. The white soldiers had come to the village again, returning with the same talk of moving the Cherokee to a new land out west...beyond the great river...and had promised new homes for the Cherokee.

The soldiers had come the first time with the message of moving them from their land. But the Cherokee of the village had ignored the talk, and had continued to live undisturbed in their settlement, making no preparations to leave their homeland.

White Feather believed that the talk of immigration by the soldiers was a threat to entice her people to go voluntarily to the new Indian Territory as some of the Cherokee people had already done years before. Then the white people invading their lands could satisfy their greed and take more Cherokee land for themselves.

"But," thought White Feather, "it is only talk from the white soldiers."

She paused, removed her hands from the cow, straightened her back to rest for a moment, and then leaned over and continued the milking chore.

"Why do the white people want more land? They have taken so much of our lands already. When will they stop?" she thought with a frown. "True, our land is beautiful, filled with mountains, rivers, streams and animals in the thick forests, but our village is small and the white people have much land. We Cherokee are peaceful people; we are not trouble-makers. We tend our gardens, plow our fields, mind our own business and live in peace with our neighbors."

A frown again crossed White Feather's face. "When will the white men leave us alone?" she thought.

White Feather refused to believe that she would ever leave this land, but there were realities that she could not ignore. She knew that the white men had discovered gold in the heart of the Cherokee land some years ago and the discovery of it had caused invasion from the greedy white men who were hungry for quick fortunes. The men searching for gold had pushed their way into the Cherokee lands, had stolen Indian cattle and attacked Indian women. New devouring white settlers had continued to come, taking Indian lands from the Cherokee and encouraging the gold miners to make more trouble so the Indians would give up more of their land. Some of the white people had organized groups called Pony Clubs and the rowdy gangs had ridden into Cherokee country starting fires and plundering the homes of the Indians. These were things White Feather knew to be true, and the thoughts of them filled her with apprehension. Many of the young Cherokee had wanted to fight the trespassers, but the older Cherokee men knew that violence from the Indians would give the white government leaders the excuse they needed to send their soldiers onto Cherokee lands with many guns, perhaps killing the people.

John Ross, the recognized Principal Chief of the Cherokee Nation, had strongly advised against acts of violence. Trusting his words of caution, the Cherokee had vowed not to fight. Even as the white raiders continually drove the Cherokee away from their homes, the Indians remained peaceful and placed their trust in the hands of John Ross, who worked daily to halt the exile of his Cherokee people.

White Feather felt grateful that her small village had been spared from the harsh treatment of roving thieves. Since most of the villages falling prey to the crimes being committed by the outlaws were located along the main trails or had been the larger towns where there was much to steal, White Feather felt that her little settlement had probably been saved by its remote location. It would be difficult to find. But the soldiers had already found it.

"What...what if the raiders do find us?" she thought in sudden alarm, her hands pausing in her task. She shuddered.

Resuming her milking, her thoughts raced. "The soldiers who came to our village spoke of treaties that our people have made with their government. Yes, I know of the treaties that have been broken by the white men, where more of our land was taken away. Once our Cherokee Nation had much land...the treaties made have not been honored." She paused. "Now the white government promises money if we go away...beyond the great river." She shook her head in disgust.

"NO!" she said aloud, anger rising in her throat, startling the cow, who swung her head around to look at White Feather. "I do not wish to have the white government's money. Let them keep their money. This is my home!"

Long before they married, White Feather and Running Deer had chosen the small tract of land by the river for their cabin. Together they had labored long days, sometimes into the night, clearing the spot where their home would sit on a gentle rise facing the river. They had built the one-room cabin themselves with occasional help from their close friend, Tsu-La (Red Fox).

Surrounded by their friends, White Feather and Running Deer had been married by a visiting missionary in the church in the village. They had been content during their years of marriage, toiling continuously to make improvements to their farm, adding the barn and rail fences around the cabin.

White Feather finished milking the cow, stood up slowly, sighed, and stretched. Picking up the full bucket of milk, she walked back across the yard toward the cabin.

She entered quietly, but Little Fawn stirred on her bunk, opening her dark eyes and smiled at her mother.

"Good morning, Little Fawn," she said. Placing the milk on the board table adjacent to the stone fireplace, she went to her daughter. She lifted the child into her arms, kissing her lightly on the cheek. Carrying Little Fawn, White Feather walked to the open doorway.

The mother watched as Running Deer stood, stretched his frame to its full height, and stepped back to survey his work. Glancing toward the cabin he

lifted a hand, waving to his wife and daughter, then began walking toward them.

"All is well," White Feather said softly to her daughter.

CHAPTER TWO

A Village of Soldiers

The warm late afternoon sun lowered itself lazily in the western sky, casting shadows over the distant mountains. From within the green shadows came a lone figure.

Running Deer stood up from his chair on the porch and raised his hand in greeting to Tsu-la.

"The soldiers came back to the village this morning," Tsu-la began. "They...."

Tsu-la hesitated on the lower step, interrupted by a grunt of disgust from White Feather as she jerked her head up from her weaving to look across the river. He looked at Running Deer with questioning eyes as to whether he should resume speaking.

At the slight nod from Running Deer, Tsu-la continued. "The soldiers spoke again of our people leaving here...going like those who have already left us for the new land west of the great Mississippi. Today the soldier's words were strong and firm. When they mounted their horses to leave, one of them shouted that all of the Cherokee in the settlement should be at the meeting.'"

"A meeting?" White Feather said. "What kind of meeting?"

"They're going to return in two days for a meeting to to tell us about the move and how we should get ready...and when."

"Leave? Well, I'm not going to leave," snapped White Feather.

Tsu-la watched the frown on White Feather's brow. He greatly disliked bringing news that upset White Feather, especially in her condition.

"Go on, Tsu-la," urged Running Deer. "Is there more?"

"Maybe the soldiers are right! The people of our village should get ready to leave."

Hearing these words from Tsu-la, White Feather's body trembled with rage. "How can you suggest such a thing?" Her voice broke.

"The soldiers said.... " Tsu-la began again.

"I don't want to hear any more of what the soldiers said," White Feather interrupted once more. Setting her basket down, she attempted to rise from her stool, but the clumsiness of her weighted body caused her to fall back.

Running Deer stood and helped her. He looked into her eyes, softly patting her shoulder.

"I must go," said Tsu-la, moving away from the anger of the woman. "Others need to know of the soldiers' words...that they are to come to the village."

At the edge of the forest, he turned and raised his hand.

"I don't want to go," White Feather said quietly, her anger leaving with Tsu-la.

Running Deer picked up his knife, sat down and resumed his work on the buckeye-wood bear he was carving for Little Fawn. "Where do you not want to go?" he said, looking at her sideways.

"To the meeting in the village. I do not wish to hear the words of the white soldiers." She, too, sat down and resumed pushing the white oak splint through the sides of the unfinished basket.

"We must go, White Feather," Running Deer said

softly. "We must hear what our people have to say."

"I have heard the white soldiers words before...always words filled with promises of a better life for the Cherokee," she responded, pausing from her weaving. She turned her face toward Running Deer, looking deeply into his eyes. "We have a good life here. I will never leave from this land."

"Yes, I know, White Feather. We love our home here in the mountains...as do all our Cherokee brothers. We do not wish to leave the land of our ancestors." He paused, and then went on, "But we must go to the meeting. We will tell the soldiers of our feelings."

"I am not leaving," White Feather said in a determined voice. "This is my home."

"This is what we must tell the soldiers. We do not wish to leave. We are happy here. We must speak our feelings," Running Deer said gently. "We are but a small village. Perhaps they will let us stay."

"My children and generations to come should know the joy of living their lives surrounded by the beauty of their ancestral lands." Pausing in her work, White Feather's gaze went beyond her husband to the horizon. A slight smile crossed her face as the unborn child she carried beneath her heart leapt as if to affirm his mother's thoughts.

"Let the others go if they wish. I will...," she mused as if to herself, and then came a swift change, "Running Deer, the soldiers...will not drive us away from our home...will they?" a small, almost child-like voice stumbled out.

"We will go to the meeting. We will hear the soldiers' words," he said kindly, but firmly.

CHAPTER THREE

No Sleep

The full yellow moon shone brightly through the open windows of the cabin, illuminating the room to an almost daylight appearance. The slow movement of the water flowing gently over the river rocks and an owl's occasional hoot from a distant tree softly penetrated the silence. White Feather lay restlessly on her bed. She hated the sound of the owl; it was a bad omen.

White Feather had not slept. She sighed and turned her head and looked at her husband lying in the bed beside her and once again rationalized in her mind, "Running Deer will help the Cherokee tomorrow when the soldiers come. His words will make them understand. He has said he will tell them that we wish to stay in this small place in our land. We do not want the gold on our land – the gold that seems to be so important to the white man's ways. We do not want new homes in the place of the setting sun. We want to be left alone by the white man's government. When they hear Running Deer's words they will not make us leave the ancient land of our people. Surely they will not push us away to the land where we do not wish to go."

White Feather turned in the bed and willed sleep to come, but her troubled mind continued to ponder the fate of her people.

Her movement roused Running Deer from his sleep. "You are not sleeping?" he asked softly, his hand caressing her face.

"No."

Running Deer reached out and gathered White Feather into his arms in an effort to comfort her. He kissed her lightly on the brow. He had sensed White Feather's worry many times since Tsu-la had come and he had seen frowns on her face. White Feather's frequent smiles had disappeared and Running Deer missed them. It hurt him to see her so deeply troubled.

White Feather moved closer to the comforting warmth of her husband's body, but sleep would not come for the remainder of the night.

Neither did sleep return to Running Deer.

He had many worries concerning the move also, but he knew that he must be strong for his wife and daughter and for the child White Feather carried. His love for them ran deep in his heart and he wanted no harm to come to them.

The unborn baby moved slightly and Running Deer smiled as the infant's movement touched his body.

He hoped that the child would be a son. He longed for a son. He would teach him how to trap and hunt in the abundant forest, killing animals only for food. He would teach him how to fish in the mountain streams, how to swim in the river, how to love and live close to nature.

Most importantly, he wanted to teach his son, as well as Little Fawn and all his children yet to come, how to live their lives unselfishly in peace and harmony with all men.

CHAPTER FOUR

A Walk Through the Woods

White Feather arose long before the sun had awaken from its sleep behind the tall mountains. She lit a small lamp and carried it to the porch where she found Running Deer sitting quietly staring out into the darkness.

Standing behind him, she put her arms around his neck and hugged him close. "You are up early, my husband," she whispered softly.

"Yes," he said solemnly. He said no more, but White Feather knew that he was concerned about the meeting in the village.

She turned and went back inside to prepare a meal for them. After they had eaten she cooked more food and packed it in the basket they would take to the village. The village people would bring food also and they would all share the noon meal together. She now knew they must go, but her body was tired. The child she carried seemed heavier, lower in her body now and had made movement more difficult during the past few days. She knew Running Deer would be worried if he knew of her discomfort, so she had kept her feelings to herself. Perhaps, she thought, if he did know, he would want her to stay at home and not accompany him to the village. No, she had argued with herself, I will go with him. She desired to be at his side always, even if she did not want to see the soldiers.

The anger she had felt toward Tsu-la had diminished, but his words had left her feeling depressed and confused. Running Deer had also been quiet and withdrawn during the afternoon after Tsu-la had left their home.

Finishing her milking chore, White Feather picked up the bucket of milk and walked the short distance to the small spring where the milk would be stored until it was needed. She set the bucket in the cool, shallow water, replacing the springhouse's wooden cover that protected the milk.

When she returned to the cabin she found Running Deer and Little Fawn waiting for her on the porch. She stood silently at the foot of the steps and watched as Running Deer lifted Little Fawn into his arms and picked up the basket of food White Feather had left on the porch before going to the barn.

White Feather took a deep breath when she and Running Deer approached the trail leading to the village for she knew that the actual journey to the meeting had really begun.

The walk through the woods began in silence, each lost in his own thoughts. Deep in their hearts they both knew that the decision would not be made by the Cherokee, but would be made by the leaders of the white government.

CHAPTER FIVE

The New Echota Treaty

White Feather loved the short walk to the village, especially in the springtime. She enjoyed the sight of the wild flowers and tall green trees surrounding the trail, but today she did not notice them. She did not see the blooming wild honeysuckle that climbed the tree trunks at the edge of the path or smell the wonderful fragrance of it's blossoms. She walked along the path beside her husband in silence, her eyes cast downward, not seeing the beauty of the wild daisies and violets she loved.

Running Deer carried Little Fawn in one arm and the basket of food in the other hand. With each step the husband became more and more concerned by White Feather's downcast eyes and her slow, labored pace. Every few steps he turned a worried look in the direction of his wife.

They had been walking only a short distance when the path made a sharp turn and White Feather's foot slipped, almost causing her knees to buckle.

"Do you need to stop and rest for a while?" Running Deer asked gently.

"No," she answered, forging ahead.

The young couple and their child continued in silence.

When they rounded the last bend in the path, the village came into view, bustling with people of the settlement.

"Shi-yo, shi-yo (hello)," came the greetings of many friends. "We are glad to see you."

White Feather and Running Deer laughed and talked with their friends and the white soldiers were momentarily forgotten.

Running Deer took the basket of food to the long table beside the river where other baskets had been placed. Then he sat Little Fawn down and moved away to speak to some Cherokee men nearby. White Feather took the child's hand and moved to a group of her women neighbors and stood listening to the conversations. She expected the talk to be of the white soldiers' meeting, but the women spoke of other things. It was as if the soldiers were not a reality to them. Her gaze scanned the large assemblage of people; there were no soldiers.

"White Feather! White Feather!"

Turning, White Feather saw Sunflower hurrying toward her with her little girl in her arms. The young women had been close childhood friends and had grown even closer as they grew into womanhood.

Sunflower had married and later had a child almost on the same day as White Feather. Sunflower had kept Little Fawn in her home many times so the girls could play together and give White Feather some rest during her pregnancy.

Sunflower put her child down beside Little Fawn and hugged White Feather. "How are you feeling? Is the time close for the little one?" she smiled, patting White Feather's swollen belly.

"No, not yet...but soon, I hope."

"Let's sit over here," Sunflower began, taking White Feather's arm and guiding her away from the group to a large log nearby. The children followed their mothers to where they sat, then moved off to play nearby.

White Feather truly loved Sunflower, but she could not discuss the removal because her friend favored the move to the western territory. She knew Sunflower had an adventurous streak in her, but White Feather could not understand why she would want to leave. The last time she and Sunflower had discussed the removal they had fringed on quarreling and White Feather had changed the subject to avoid having bad feelings between them. Today the women talked and laughed about more pleasant things.

After Running Deer left White Feather he had found his friend Tsu-la with the Cherokees, and the two walked to a large circle of men gathered in the cool shade under a tall hemlock tree by the river.

Unlike the women, the men within the group were speaking of the white government and the removal. Their conversations were filled with anxious remarks and unanswered questions. Many of the men were confused, expressing anger or they were asking questions that had not been addressed by the soldiers on their visit to the village two days ago.

Running Deer and Tsu-la stood listening attentively to the men for a while, considering their words of concern about the movement of their people, but soon Tsu-la could not resist joining in the talk.

"When the soldiers came they spoke of the treaty made at our Cherokee capital in New Echota,"

"What kind of treaty?" said a young Cherokee man. "Another one to be broken?"

"A treaty made between the Cherokee and the white president, Andrew Jackson," Tsu-la continued. "Our people here in our village know of the treaty."

"I know of the treaty...we all do," spoke an angry voice, "one signed by a handful of our Cherokee people."

"Yes, but the white government says it is legal. They...."

"Legal? Hah!" came a voice within the crowd.

"And where was our chief, John Ross, when some of our people signed their names? He was not present in New Echota!" He paused briefly. "Did he know about the meeting?" Without waiting for an answer he rushed on. "No! I heard he was sitting in a jail in Tennessee...put there by Georgia Guards who had no reason to arrest him. It was a trick to keep him from attending the meeting!"

"Yes, how could he speak for us...he wasn't there," added another.

"The treaty is a fraud!" a young Cherokee furiously added.

The men turned to each other expressing their feelings, declaring the treaty to be trickery.

Tsu-la looked around the men and raised his voice again to be heard. "Wait!" he said, appealing with outstretched arms. "The soldiers have told us that many of our people have already gone to the new land." Then, lowering his voice, he added, "Perhaps we too must go."

"NO! NO! NO! NEVER! NO!" the men's voices echoed through the crowd becoming louder and louder. Some of the other villagers nearby paused from talking and turned to look at the men in alarm.

Running Deer had remained silent, listening to the words of the Cherokee men, considering all that had been said. He stepped forward. "Wait!" his voice demanding to be heard. "Wait! Let us tell the soldiers of the feelings here in our small village. The soldiers will hear the words of our people."

Tsu-la moved to stand beside his friend. "The soldiers say we have no choice," he persisted. "The soldiers say their government has orders to force us to leave our land and go to the new Indian Territory."

"NO! NO! NEVER!" the protesters' voices resounded again and again. A few of the men turned and walked away in anger.

Running Deer calmly raised his voice above the din of words around him. He wanted to be careful how he spoke, least the Indians misconstrue his remarks, for he did not want them to think he sided with the invaders. "Let us hear the words of the soldiers," he pleaded, looking at the men, scanning each face, asking for patience. "We need to hear what the treaty says."

"The white soldiers are many...with guns," Tsu-la said. "Lives of our people could be lost if we refuse to go. Let us not forget that."

"We will frighten our women and children with our loud voices," spoke Running Deer quietly. "Let's wait and hear the soldiers' words."

His wisdom quieted the men. Each one somberly glanced around at the women and children, their Cherokee families and friends, thoughtfully considering what he has said. Then Running Deer dropped his head and walked away from the group with a heavy heart. The message of the soldiers would not be new to him. He had already heard the news from Tsu-la the day before.

Suddenly a slight commotion arose from within the assembly and then all grew quiet except for the voices of the playing children. Horse hooves on the road leading into the village penetrated the silence. When the soldiers came into view, the children were instantly frightened by the strange men on horses carrying guns; they ran to cling to their mothers' skirts.

White Feather arose from the log and looked directly at the men as they came closer. She watched as the soldiers dismounted and tethered their horses to the trees by the path. Straightening her shoulders, she felt confident that Running Deer would speak for their people.

In her mind ran the story of the New Echota fraudulent treaty. She knew that John Ross, friend of the Cherokee and their leader, had made many efforts during the past years to help the Cherokee remain on their land. He had made countless trips to the white capital in Washington City to speak to the white government leaders for his people. After the New Echota treaty had been signed and following his release from jail, John Ross had presented congressmen and senators with a petition bearing more than 5,000 Cherokee signatures denouncing the fraudulent document. No, White Feather would not give up hope unless it was absolutely necessary. "Perhaps John Ross will come today to speak to the soldiers on behalf of his people of this village," White Feather thought hopefully.

But John Ross would not be present in White Feather's village today, and Running Deer's words would not change the minds of the soldiers. All could see that the soldiers had orders from their government.

News traveled slowly in the mountains of the Cherokee land and the people of White Feather's small remote village did not know that John Ross's tireless efforts to keep the Cherokee on their land had failed. The Cherokee leader had not been able to resist the overwhelming force of the white government and despite his efforts, the white senate had ratified the treaty on May 23, 1836, giving the Cherokee two years in which to move to the new territory.

CHAPTER SIX

The Captain

Adozen or so soldiers finished tethering their horses in the trees on each side of the path. Pulling their rifles from the sides of their saddles, they positioned their barrels over their shoulders and formed a single line in front of the military man who was in charge. Satisfied that the men were ready, he turned toward the people and led the line of soldiers through the Cherokee. The Indians silently parted to let them pass.

The soldier in command walked up to the top step of the church entrance where he could be seen and heard by everyone present. The soldiers formed a large circle around the villagers. Moving their rifles from their shoulders they held them in both hands in front of their bodies and spread their feet apart in a resting position. They stared at the Cherokee with motionless faces, their eyes gravitating to the slightest movement in the crowd and held their rifles as threats of preparation for resistance should it occur during the meeting.

"Cherokee," the soldier on the steps spoke loudly, "I am Captain Howard," he began. "I have been sent to your village today on behalf of the United States government. I am pleased that you have come to the meeting. Come closer so that all of you may hear the message I have brought to you from my government."

Responding to his words Running Deer and White Feather moved to the front of the church while the others followed slowly behind them, their faces lined with dreaded anticipation.

Waiting for the captain to speak again, White Feather turned to look at the circle of soldiers as the uniformed men moved in closer, surrounding the Cherokee.

"This is not right," she thought. "We are peaceful people. We mean no harm. We wish only to be left alone." She shuddered slightly at the sight of armed soldiers surrounding her people.

Running Deer felt the tremor and released her hand and put a protective arm around her shoulders, gently pulling her close to his side. He felt the tremor again and he pulled her even closer to him.

"Thank you," said the captain, looking over the faces of the Indians. "The message I bring to you today concerns the removal of the Cherokee Indians to the new Indian territory in the west. The New Echota treaty, signed by your people and my government in 1828, states that..."

"The treaty is a fraud," a young Cherokee man's voice loudly interrupted. "A small number of our people were tricked into signing it."

Encouraged by the outburst from his Cherokee brother another young man shouted, "Our Principal Chief, John Ross, signed no such treaty. Our leader was not present when the treaty was signed."

At the outbursts from the Indian men the soldiers moved in closer.

Running Deer, dropped his arm from White Feather's shoulders and turned to the villagers. "Wait!" he said loudly. Swinging back around, he stepped forward to address the captain. Speaking in a calm voice, he looked straight into the captain's face and asked, "What does the treaty say?"

The captain had waited patiently while the Cherokee men had expressed their anger concerning the treaty and had made no effort to interrupt them. Now all eyes fell on the captain.

The mere mention of the detested treaty brought an angry outburst from the Cherokee, but now they became eager to hear what the captain would say.

"The treaty says," began the captain, "that the Cherokee Nation ceded, relinquished and conveyed to the United States all the lands owned, claimed or possessed by the Nation east of the Mississippi River."

Sounds of disagreement interrupted the captain and a few of the Indians disgustedly turned their backs on him.

"And for the land, five million dollars is to be paid to the Cherokee."

More disgruntled murmurs fell on the captain's ears as he scanned the Indians' faces and raised his voice in an attempt to be heard.

"In exchange for your land here, the Cherokee people will receive additional western lands."

"We will not leave. The whites must leave," a rebellious young Cherokee man yelled.

Captain Howard considered his audience. He had heard reports at the fort from a Georgia spy who had traveled across the Cherokee Nation recently for Georgia Governor Gilmer. The spy had reported that he had seen many of the Cherokee building new cabins, mending their fences and preparing their fields for planting. Their normal daily activity had continued as though there was no thought of leaving their homes.

"Perhaps this settlement of Indians also had hopes of a new treaty that would allow them to remain on their land," the captain thought as he looked at the Cherokee near him. The spy had also related seeing Indians carrying corn into the mountains where they would try to hide and avoid capture by the federal soldiers. As the captain's gaze moved across the faces of the villagers he could not imagine what these people would actually do, but he was certain that none of them would go voluntarily to the west.

The citizens of Georgia were reportedly disturbed by the Indians' attitude of defiance, but the captain couldn't blame the Cherokee. Sadly he thought of the days ahead when the federal troops would arrive and force them from their homes.

The captain felt deep compassion and sympathy for the Cherokee and he respected their feelings. A good military man, he served the army in a professional manner, but he could not agree with the removal of the Indians from their homes. He hoped his military enlistment would be ended before the actual roundup and march to the west began. He felt that the removal was wrong and he wanted no part of it. These feelings ran deep, but he would keep them to himself, at least while he served the United States Army.

The captain paused, wishing that the people standing near him knew how much he despised bringing them the message of removal.

Running Deer stepped forward, now even closer to the captain, and spoke pleadingly. "We hear the message you have brought, but our land is small. We do not wish new land or your government's money. Let us stay here in the home of our people."

Ignoring Running Deer's pleas, the captain looked over his head and addressed the people. "The United States has given the Cherokee two years in which to leave their land and go to the new territory west of the Mississippi River. Over one year has passed. Many of your people have already gone. Now the people of your village must prepare to go also."

Words of protest resounded through the crowd.

"We have orders for you to leave immediately," Captain Howard continued, his voice rising firmly above the people.

"Whose orders?" questioned one of the elders of the village.

"The United States government," replied the

captain. "We do not wish bloodshed. We want no one killed, but our orders are that you come peacefully. If not, then our government will force you to leave with many guns."

Some of the villagers stood frozen, unable to comprehend. More were becoming restless and angry at the directness of the captain's words. Others dropped their heads, silent tears forming in their eyes, reflecting resignation of the fate they feared, but hoped would not come to them.

White Feather stood motionless, staring at the captain, too numb to shed tears. She knew in her heart that she would never leave her home. "I will not leave," she said, her words spoken so softly that only those standing close by could hear them.

She heard Running Deer's voice and she looked to see that he had moved up onto the bottom step with Little Fawn still in his arms.

"We are but a small group of Cherokee. We mind our own business and live in peace. Surely your government will let this small village of people remain on the land of our fathers. Let us continue on...." he pleaded again.

"All of the Cherokee must go," the captain replied sympathetically.

"There are people in our village who are old, some are too sick to be moved. They cannot make such a trip of which you speak. What will happen to them?" Running Deer continued.

Before the captain could reply, other voices rose.

"What will happen to our homes, our barns, our livestock, our...."

"How will we travel to the new land?"

"What will happen to our Cherokee lands after we leave?"

The captain raised his hands in front of him as a sign for the people to be quiet and listen.

"All the Cherokee must go," he repeated. "You will be paid for your land and property. The United States government will take care of you on the trip, will give you food and will provide for your needs for one full year after you get to the new land."

"How much for a barn, livestock and...."

Captain Howard interrupted. "Each of you will be paid fifty-six dollars and thirty-eight cents."

The villagers were all quietly speaking at once among themselves, reflecting on their uncertainty.

The soldiers now had their weapons aimed toward the Cherokee, ready for anything.

White Feather stood immobilized, staring at the captain, disbelief etched on her face. She felt the pain as her heart seemed to crack into small pieces from fear and grief.

Running Deer moved to White Feather, holding her and Little Fawn close to him in an effort to comfort them, but could not speak. There were no words he could say that would erase the finality of the Captain's words.

White Feather looked up into Running Deer's face and whispered in a broken voice, "Thank you, Running Deer, thank you for trying."

"Cherokee, please listen to me," Captain Howard said in a compassionate voice. He raised his arms in an attempt to gain attention and said, "I have further orders from my government."

Voices flared from the crowd of angry Cherokee.

"You must listen to me and understand. You do not have a choice. This is an order from the United States government," he added firmly.

"The United States government – hah!" mumbled a young Cherokee.

"Begin at once to prepare to leave," the Captain continued, "Those of you who are ready tomorrow may leave then. Soldiers will be back to escort you to join others who will be leaving from Indian settlements to travel west. The rest of you must prepare to leave soon."

He walked slowly down the steps and when he passed White Feather and Running Deer he paused in front of them and looked at the family. He touched Little Fawn lightly on the shoulder and looked deeply into White Feather's troubled eyes for a quick moment, then moved on without saying a word. He, with the other soldiers following him, left the settlement as quickly as they had entered.

Suddenly, the truth quieted all voices.

The stunned Cherokee stood too shocked to move or speak as the impact of the words they had heard in the brief meeting began to penetrate their thoughts.

The captain had announced what they had feared most.

When the sound of hooves could no longer be heard and the dust had settled on the road, the Cherokee began turning to each other. Anger had been replaced by doubts, uncertainties, disbelief and decisions that must be made.

Tsu-la had stood quietly in the back while the captain spoke. It pained him to see his people suffering. Now he walked to the front to stand on the top step at the church.

His voice, loud but kind, captured their attention. "We need help for our people. We need hospitals, churches and schools for our children. Can a small handful of Cherokee fight the many white soldiers who will come?" Then, lowering his voice, he added, "We should prepare to leave for the new land as soon as possible."

White Feather, shocked at her friend's words, looked at him in disbelief. "Tsu-la, what are you saying? Do you want to leave our land?" she asked.

"Can we fight the whole state of Georgia and the United States government? We have no choice," he said sadly. He was silent for a moment, then raised his head, looked out across his people and softly added, "I will go tomorrow with the others."

White Feather gasped. "NO!" she whispered.

Running Deer tightened his arm around White Feather.

"No," she whispered to Running Deer.

Tsu-la saw the disbelief and hurt on his friends'

faces, and he dropped his head, turned and walked slowly away from his people, heading toward the river.

His decision to leave had been made long before the soldiers arrived today. He would leave tomorrow for the land beyond the great river, and there he would begin a new life for himself. What kind of life, he had no idea, but his decision was final. Perhaps, he thought, there in new surroundings, he could build new, good memories. He would leave all his sad memories behind him.

CHAPTER SEVEN

Tsu-la's Decision

Tsu-la's labored steps brought him to the river's edge. He stood by its side for a moment, then sighed and sank down wearily onto the soft grass beside the water.

He gazed out across the river. "My people feel I am wrong to leave our land tomorrow. They do not know the true feelings of my heart. I must go. White Feather will understand someday, I am sure," he thought sadly.

The decision to leave had not come easily to Tsu-la as some of his people might think. The decision had been a very difficult one to make.

Tsu-la had pondered over the removal of his people since the first appearance of the soldiers in the village. He knew that he could never be happy here again without his life's companion. He would go to the land of the setting sun, far away from the only home he had ever known, begin a new life and attempt to find happiness for himself again. Accepting the knowledge that many difficulties and hardships would lie ahead for him, Tsu-la still felt that this was what he must do. His decision had been made and it would not be changed--now nor tomorrow.

He raised his slumped shoulders, sighed and straightened his back. He looked out at the moving water pouring over the rocks in the river. His eyes focused on the river and finally rested on a small quiet pool of water trapped between several huge rocks. In the pool he saw the vision of her face, smiling up at him, the face that constantly lived in his mind. He shuddered, took a deep breath and closed his eyes. He could not remove her from his thoughts. He had made many attempts, but Tsu-la could not release the wife he loved. The familiar surroundings of this home-land held her memories everywhere he looked or ventured to roam, even into the deepest woods where he often went to be alone.

Graceful, Morning Star moved like a fawn in every vision of her he encountered. Now she was gone forever from his life, but her face kept returning to him. "Morning Star," he whispered, opening his eyes to see that the vision had disappeared. "My Morning Star."

For two summers Morning Star had been all his...time that had filled Tsu-la's life with complete happiness. She had been a healthy, happy young woman who had brought much joy into his life until the morning when he had watched her close her eyes and quietly die in his arms.

The morning of her death Running Deer had come to Tsu-la's cabin just after sunrise to go hunting with his friend, and he had found Tsu-la holding his wife.

Following her burial, Tsu-la had become silent, never speaking or smiling. At Running Deer's constant insistence Tsu-la had slowly begun nourishing his body again. Tsu-la stayed in his cabin alone, not wishing to see anyone, including Running Deer, but every day his friend kept returning, bringing food White Feather prepared, insisting that Tsu-la eat. Sitting daily by his grieving friend, Running Deer was unaware that Tsu-la had sunk so deeply into depression until late one afternoon when he entered Tsu-la's cabin.

"Tsu-la, how are you?" Running Deer said in deep concern.

Tsu-la did not respond.

Running Deer hurried to the table where Tsu-la sat slumped over the small table in the center of the room.

Running Deer, shocked that Tsu-la was not responding, put his hands on Tsu-la's shoulders and said, "Come...come home with me."

"No."

"Yes. When have you eaten last?"

"I don't know. I'm not hungry."

"Come, get up. You are coming home with me. White Feather will feed you and we will talk."

Tsu-la protested, but Running Deer pulled him up and was finally able to persuade Tsu-la to go home with him.

White Feather and Little Fawn were delighted to see Tsu-la. Smiling briefly, Tsu-la lifted Little Fawn into his arms and the child hugged and kissed him.

Tsu-la spoke little during the meal, answering only when White Feather or Running Deer directed a question to him, but his friends were glad to see that he did eat well.

After supper the men retired to the porch. They talked late into the night, long after White Feather had gone to bed.

The long evening of talking with Running Deer resulted in Tsu-la's acceptance of Morning Star's death and the realization that his life must continue without her. He promised Running Deer that he would try to change his behavior.

Shortly after sunrise the next morning, he began his day by planting a garden, working until exhaustion overcame his body late in the afternoon. He filled the following days by hunting game in the forest, fishing in the river, walking in the woods and visiting with his friends in the village.

One day as Tsu-la walked out of his cabin to leave to go hunting, the soldiers came with news of the removal and Tsu-la listened closely to their words. The military men came back several weeks later and Tsu-la again listened to their message. When the soldiers returned the third time, Tsu-la had secretly made his final decision about his future. He felt that if he left his home in the mountains and went to the new territory he would be forced to begin a new life, no matter how difficult the unknown land might present itself. Without the familiar surroundings perhaps he could leave the sad memories far behind. It would be a difficult struggle, but it seemed the only solution to preserve his life and find new happiness. Most importantly, he was sure that his Cherokee brothers would join him in the new Indian Territory in the near future. The move was inescapable.

"Yes, I will go tomorrow. The other Cherokee will follow soon," he thought sadly as he glanced over his shoulder at the village people in the distance.

"No, White Feather," he silently answered the question she had asked him before he had walked away from the village meeting and not answered. "I do not wish to leave our land here. You do not understand. I must go."

Tsu-la breathed a deep sigh as he pulled his weary body up from the ground. He stood for a brief moment and looked at the sparkling water. His gaze moved back to the tranquil pool where he had seen the image of Morning Star.

"I will always love you, Morning Star. I will never forget you," he whispered. "But now, I go to the west."

CHAPTER EIGHT

Going Home

The late afternoon sun filtered through the tall trees and cast its warmth on the Cherokee family as they moved slowly along the path leading home.

White Feather, carrying the empty food basket, and Running Deer, with Little Fawn sleeping on his shoulder, walked in silence. The sadness they held in their hearts had overwhelmed them. Only the couple's soft footsteps and the occasional sound of birds singing in the nearby trees shifted the quietness of the still afternoon.

It had been a long day for White Feather, the young Indian woman hot and miserable. The gentle breeze failed to cool her warm body. Frowning she wiped the moisture from her brow. She would be glad when they arrived at their peaceful home after the grueling day in the village.

Defeat shadowed her footsteps as she thought of the young captain's words. Oddly she thought that the captain had not been unkind to them when he performed the task he had been assigned to accom-

plish.   After reflecting on his demeanor during the
meeting, she had sensed that he had not been pleased
to bring the final orders of the removal. When he had
paused before her during his departure, he had looked
compassionately into her eyes as if searching for for-
giveness.   As he turned to walk away he had touched
Little Fawn lightly on the shoulder and smiled. White
Feather wondered if the young captain was remembering his own child and family. She felt no anger toward
the military man personally for she knew that he did
not have the authority to allow the Cherokee to remain
in Georgia. Her anger toward him faded.

"The captain brought sadness to my people,"
she thought; this she would never forget. Her eyes
clouded with fresh tears and she stumbled, almost
falling to the ground.

"White Feather!" Running Deer said, alarmed by
her near fall. "Let us stop for you to rest."

Straightening, she answered in a whisper, "No, I
want to get home. I will rest later."

Running Deer wanted to touch her, but instead
the family continued on their journey toward the
cabin in silence, with Running Deer worriedly glancing
often at his wife.

White Feather caught her breath quickly when
she felt another sharp pain pierce into her back.
There had been many pains today.

"Maybe," she thought wearily, "the time for the
baby to come is to be soon." White Feather glanced
out of the corners of her eyes toward her husband.
Running Deer had cared for her during the torturous
day, at the same time taking care of Little Fawn.

Running Deer had left White Feather's side only
for a short time during the afternoon to share words
with Tsu-la. When he returned, he tried to speak
about their conversation, but she had not responded,
even when he told her that others in the village had
planned to leave the next day, including Sunflower
and her family.

"Well, let them go if they wish," she had
thought.

After the soldiers had left the village, White Feather heard some of her friends' ploy to elude the soldiers by escaping into the mountains, "We could do this also...then, when the soldiers return," she mused, "we will be gone. They will never find us in the land we know so well. But...if they go, we will never see Tsu-la, or Sunflower or any of our friends again." At the thought, she moaned.

Her mind now on Tsu-la, White Feather remembered how much he had changed since the death of Morning Star. He had become a different person, always sad, never smiling and rarely visiting with his friends of the settlement. He seemed so lonely.   Time will help him to heal she knew, but the old Tsu-la was gone.

White Feather sighed. How she missed the lively Morning Star! They had shared much together. Morning Star had been with White Feather to help her with the birth of Little Fawn. Running Deer and Tsu-la had waited anxiously on the porch. The four friends had shed tears of joy when Little Fawn arrived.

When Morning Star had become ill, Running Deer and White Feather had been extremely worried about her, but they thought, as did Tsu-la, that she would become well again. Young and healthy, she would overcome the illness. White Feather had been sure.

She remembered how Tsu-la had been at his wife's bedside constantly during the days of her illness. Then the medicine man from the Indian village north of them came with herbs and medicines for Morning Star, and she was taken to the sweat lodge. Songs were sung, prayers were said, but the fever in Morning Star's body had continued to rise. She died in her sleep just before dawn at the end of her third day of sickness.

"Yes," thought White Feather, "Tsu-la has never been the same since Morning Star's death. Now he wants to leave our land." She shook her head. She wished happiness for Tsu-la, but it remained difficult for her to believe that he would leave tomorrow. She sighed and moved her head again in wonder. Another deep pain struck across her back; she flinched. "It will soon be time for the baby."

Running Deer's thoughts were also on Tsu-la. They had shared much together, but Running Deer could not share this move to a new land with Tsu-la. He, like his wife, would never choose to leave the land of their ancestors.

The cabin came into view in the distance. He felt gladness. He wanted White Feather to rest.

"White Feather," he said softly, "we are home. Look at our chimney...the spirit of the fire is still standing guard."

White Feather lifted her head and then smiled. "Home," she said softly.

CHAPTER NINE

Looking In The Mirror

Captain Howard stared at the road in front of him. He despised bringing the final orders from his government that would soon uproot these people from their homes. This assignment had proved to be the most difficult he had encountered during his years of military service.

"It is wrong," he thought grimly. "They were here first."

When his orders had arrived assigning him as one of the officers to oversee the removal, he had been unhappy, and today, that unhappiness grew. He squinted his eyes toward the hot sun, and then leaned over to get his water canteen. His throat burned and, turning the canteen up, he drank deeply of the water.

As he returned the flask to its place, he sighed, pushing his heels into the sides of the horse. He wanted to arrive back at the fort in time to rest. Suddenly, he remembered the dance scheduled for tonight! He loved dancing and this would probably be the last one he would attend for a long time. His date for the evening was Colonel Harris' daughter and he knew her company would be pleasant. He wanted to enjoy himself, but how could he forget about the Cherokee and their sadness.

"Forget?" he silently questioned himself. Faces of the Cherokee family returned to him again as he stared at the road in front of him...the husband holding a little girl and the wife carrying her unborn child.

The young couple had stood near him while he addressed the villagers. They had touched his heart, their devotion to each other obvious. The husband had bravely stepped forward, pleading for his people and Captain Howard had admired his courage. The young Indian woman, heavy with child, had affected him in a way that no woman had before. She was beautiful.

The captain looked up to see the fort on the horizon. He straightened, attempting to release all thoughts. He began to prepare his report of the day's activities to his commanding officer in his head.

The sun was setting in the western sky when Michael entered the room he shared with his friend, Lieutenant Sterling.

"How was your day, Captain?" Sterling said.

Captain Howard shrugged, but did not answer.

"You look exhausted."

"Well, the ride was long and dusty. I'm glad to be back." The captain removed his hat and coat, then went to the washstand and splashed his face with cool water. Absently, he looked at his reflection in the dull mirror, patting his weary face with a cloth. Then, taking the bowl to the porch, he tossed out the water, glancing back toward the mountains in the direction of the Indian village he had visited earlier. He returned slowly to the room and went to his bunk and fell down across it, lying on his back with his arm flung across his eyes.

"What's wrong with you tonight, Captain? You've been looking forward to this dance for days. Are you sick?"

"No." He got up, bathed, shaved and began to

dress for the evening's affair.

Sterling remained silent, watching Captain Howard, worried because his friend seemed to be so troubled. "I hate to push, Buddy," he began good-naturedly, "but are you sure you're not sick?"

"No...I'm not sick!"

"Well, what's the matter? It's just not like you to be so quiet."

After a moment of silence Captain Howard paused from dressing, sank down on his cot and looked straight at his friend. "I can't stop thinking about the Cherokee who will be forced to leave their homes," he said somberly.

"The Indians?"

"Yes."

"Why should you worry about the Indians?"

Captain Howard stood, thrust his hands deep into his pockets, and began to pace the floor. He told his friend the events that had occurred in the village and of his compassion toward the Indians. He stopped his pacing and sat down upon his cot.

Sterling listened intently, bewildered by the words. "Aw, they're just Indians," he said, turning to look in the mirror himself and combing his hair. "They belong in the new territory. We'll get them out there and they'll be happy again with their own people." He laughed, irritating Michael.

"No! They have no desire to be forced from their homes and driven like cattle across the river and into the west." Michael rose to his feet.

"But when we get them out of Georgia, we will have more room for the white settlers," said Sterling lightly.

"It is wrong to take their land from them!" Anger rose in Michael's voice as he walked solidly toward the door.

"Captain, you worry too much about those Indians. Sometimes I think you must be part Indian yourself," Sterling chuckled, picking up his coat from his cot.

Michael paused, his hand resting on the door

handle. He turned and shot a look at the army officer across the room. "If I were, I'd be proud of it!" he said.

Sterling's fingers hesitated in the buttoning of his uniform, startled at the words he had heard and stared in disbelief at the Captain.

"You can't be serious," he said.

"Yes...yes I can!" Michael opened the door and left the room.

Walking away, the Captain's lips moved silently with his thoughts, "How could I have been so wrong about a man?"

CHAPTER TEN

The Fate of the People

Tsu-la dressed and glanced around the room before leaving the small cabin that had been his home for years. He sighed, dreading to visit his friends for the last time. His belongings had been given away, except for the few that he would carry in his arms. A young couple in the village to be wed in the next few days would soon use the cabin. "Perhaps they will be as happy here as I once was long ago," he thought.

He spent the morning visiting and then his steps took him toward the graves of his forefathers and Morning Star. He paused at grave after grave remembering how each had affected his life. His gaze rested on a slight rise where Morning Star had been laid to rest and his steps quickened to reach the site. There, he dropped to his knees.

"Morning Star," he whispered, his eyes misty. "Our desire was to grow old together, with many children and grandchildren. Now...much has changed."

Reluctantly he rose. "Morning Star, I will always love you," he said aloud, removing a buckskin strap from his neck to lay on her grave. "I go now to talk to your mother, Moon Face."

Tsu-la had purposefully prolonged the time of bidding farewell to the older Indian woman who had been as a mother to him for more years than he could remember. Leaving Moon Face behind had plagued Tsu-la's thoughts many times following his decision to depart from his homeland.

Morning Star had been Moon Face's only child. She had been born the year before Moon Face's husband had gone away to fight the Creek Indians with Andrew Jackson over fifteen years ago. He had died in the Battle of Horseshoe Bend. When Morning Star and Tsu-la wed, Moon Face had been pleased, hoping that the union would produce many grandchildren.

Moon Face had not attended the meeting with the soldiers, but she understood Tsu-la's desire to leave. Only the look in her eyes told him when he talked of his decision, for she said nothing, even when he begged her to come with him. Now he must bid her goodbye, unless he could change her mind.

"Come with me tomorrow," he said seriously once again when Moon Face embraced him.

"No," she softly answered, shaking her head.

"The soldiers will come again," he gently reminded her.

"Yes," she answered, looking up at Tsu-la, "they will come back."

"Come with us now," Tsu-la begged.

"No. I am an old woman. It is not possible."

"I beg you to come," Tsu-la pleaded.

"No, Tsu-la," she said once again as she sat down at the small table in the middle of the room. She motioned for him to sit beside her. "I am tired. My years are too many to travel the long journey of which you speak."

"I will be there to care for you," Tsu-la assured her.

"No. You must go without me," she said with finality.

Tsu-la dropped his head, disappointed, and Moon Face placed her hand on his to comfort him.

"You are young. Go, make a new life. Our old life is gone. Go. Find happiness again," the old woman requested. "I will remain in the land of my ancestors."

Tsu-la lifted his head, resigned to Moon Face's wishes and spoke no more of the journey. She had unselfishly finalized his decision.

He rose from the table and embraced his mother-in-law.

"Go! Find a new life! Be happy." She managed a slight smile for his sake.

Tsu-la turned away, too full of emotion to respond with words, and walked slowly out of the cabin, directing his feet toward the river; he knew he could find comfort in the sound of its flow. He did not look back at Moon Face, the only mother he had ever known. His downcast eyes were clouded with tears.

Moon Face followed Tsu-la to the door and stood watching him until he disappeared. She entered the cabin, broken hearted, laid down on her bed and cried.

When Tsu-la reached the river he found a secluded spot, surrounded by large clumps of mountain laurel. He sank down on a large rock nestled in the edge of the water. As he sat, he pondered the fate of Moon Face and his people.

The elders in the village...how would they endure the future? Moon Face's husband was only one of the Cherokee men who did not return to the village after fighting the Creek Indians for the white government. Running Deer and White Feather's fathers had also died at Horseshoe Bend. Jackson had promised the Cherokee land in exchange for support in the battle, but he lied. Now Jackson had turned his back on the Cherokee, banishing them from their lands. Many of the old men of the village had helped Jackson defeat the Creek Indians and now, in return,

Jackson was forcing them to leave their homes forever.

He remembered the talk of some of the villagers' plans to escape into the mountains and hide from the soldiers when they returned.

"They will not survive the cold winters," he thought. "And food? The game in the forest is sparse. They will not have meat...no gardens, no fish. There is no way for the Cherokee to escape the wrath of the white government laws. It is useless for them to consider such a thing," Tsu-la sighed heavily. He must now bid his friends, Running Deer and White Feather, a final farewell.

And then...a distant scream interrupted his thoughts as it echoed through the quiet woods. Tsu-la listened. "Is it an animal cry?" he thought. And then, there it was again, distant but potent.

"That is not the sound of an animal," he thought as he jumped up. "It is the scream of a human voice." He began to run as the cry came again, this time he was sure that the sounds had come from the direction of Running Deer's cabin. When the next scream pierced the air Tsu-la picked up speed, the agonizing cries pushing him down the path.

When he turned the bend Running Deer's cabin came into sight, but he saw no sign of his friends. The scream was nearer now and he realized that it came from inside the cabin. Tsu-la leaped up the steps and burst into the room where White Feather lay.

He froze in his tracks, startled at the sight before him in the dimness of the small room.

White Feather screamed again.

CHAPTER ELEVEN

Sadness and Gladness

White Feather lay, pale and still, on her bed. Beads of moisture rolled down her face as rapid short panting breaths interrupted her screams, sending Tsu-la to her bedside in alarm.

"White Feather! What has happened?"

She did not answer but stretched out a hand to him, crying out in agony again. Suddenly, she involuntarily pulled her bent knees up close to her chin.

Tsu-la was startled. He looked closer.

"The baby!" he cried.

Glancing around the room quickly, he saw no one. "Why is the medicine woman not here? No one is here!" he spun around. "What should I do?"

White Feather screamed.

Tsu-la leaned down close to White Feather's face. "White Feather, where is...."

Her high-pitched pant interrupted his question. "Help me, Tsu-la. No one is here!"

"Just tell me what to do." Tsu-la's calm statement erased the wild fear in White Feather's eyes. Still, as another pain hit her, she moaned loudly.

Tsu-la saw the baby's head appearing in the birth opening of White Feather's body. Quickly he leaned over and gently cradled the baby's head in his hands as it slowly emerged.

White Feather, half rising to a sitting position, cried a long, piercing scream and pushed the infant onto the bed. Then, exhausted, she lay back and closed her eyes. The baby now lay motionless in Tsu-la's strong hands.

"Cut the cord, Tsu-la."

He heard the weary words distantly, caught up in the wonder of the moment.

He laid the infant on the bed between White Feather's legs and drew his knife from his belt. He severed the lifeline between the mother and her child.

"Tie the cord," again came the soft voice. "The rawhide is at the foot of the bed. The baby hasn't cried...pick him up."

Tsu-la did as he was told. He gently lifted the baby and with a firm slap to its back brought the newborn wailing lustily into life. Tsu-la smiled. He marveled at the strength of the child as he cleaned the squirming little body. He wrapped the baby in a soft doeskin he found nearby and laid the little one close to his mother to receive nourishment.

White Feather's tired eyes opened slightly as she guided the baby's tiny mouth to her breast and then she looked up at Tsu-la standing by her bed.

"Thank you, my friend," she whispered wearily.

"A healthy, strong little Cherokee," Tsu-la responded.

"Yes," she smiled, pulling the covering away to look at the baby's plump little body. She looked up at Tsu-la.

"Running Deer will be proud."

Tsu-la leaned down close to White Feather's face and asked softly, "White Feather, where is Running Deer? And Little Fawn?"

White Feather, now deep in sleep, did not respond.

He smiled at the sight of the newborn and its

mother, and covered White Feather with a blanket.

"I have much happy news for Running Deer today," he chuckled as he left the cabin to settle himself in a chair on the porch to wait for Running Deer's return.

Suddenly Tsu-la was tired. He rubbed his eyes and leaned his head back. He had accomplished much today but his plans had not included the surprising arrival of Running Deer's child. He was glad that he had seen Running Deer's baby before he left for the new land. The birth would be remembered as the only joyous event during his final days among his people.

CHAPTER TWELVE

The Gift of Friendship

Tsu-la had not been waiting long when he spotted his friend running up the trail toward the cabin.

Running Deer began to yell loudly as he ran toward his friend. "Tsu-la! Tsu-la! White Feather...the baby?"

Tsu-la smiled and did not answer.

"The...baby..." Running Deer cried, out of breath from his run.

"Looks like you must have run all the way from wherever you've been," teased Tsu-la good-naturedly.

"Yes," Running Deer gasped between short breaths, "yes!"

Tsu-la laughed.

"White Feather...is her time near?" Running Deer questioned loudly as he bounded up the steps nearly tripping over his feet in his haste.

"They are in the cabin," Tsu-la chuckled as he rose to greet his friend.

Running Deer stopped abruptly and looked at Tsu-la in disbelief. "They?"

"Yes, they! They are in the cabin sleeping," Tsu-la repeated, grinning at Running Deer.

Running Deer strained to look into the open cabin door. "They?" he repeated, unable to comprehend his friend's surprising words.

"You have a son, Running Deer...a son," Tsu-la laughed, slapping his friend on the back. "And they are fine. Stop all your shouting...they are sleeping!"

"A son?"

"Yes. Go see for yourself," Tsu-la smiled.

Running Deer howled a shout of happiness and rushed into the cabin, leaving Tsu-la laughing. After a moment, he settled himself down in the chair and gazed at the river.

Running Deer hurried to White Feather and their son, who lay sleeping. He knelt down beside the bunk. He kissed White Feather lightly on the brow and then leaning over the infant he looked closely at his new son.

"White Feather," he said softly.

White Feather opened her eyes and smiled up at her husband. "A son, Running Deer, we have a son."

Running Deer, kissed his wife again. Joy swelled in his eyes.

"Tsu-la was here with me."

"Yes. I am glad. I am sorry I did not get back in time."

"The baby would not wait for you," she explained.

"How do you feel?"

"Tired, but I am happy. A son, Running Deer," she said, glancing down at the sleeping infant. "He looks much like you."

Running Deer smiled broadly as he stared at the sleeping infant. "Now Little Fawn has a brother. She will be happy."

"Yes," White Feather answered, trying to stay awake.

"You must rest now. Sleep," said Running Deer, gently tracing his fingers across her brow and down her cheek. "I will sit with Tsu-la while you rest."

"Yes," she answered, and closed her eyes.

Running Deer sank down on the log bench next to Tsu-la. "Thank you for your help. I am glad you were here."

"Where were you, Running Deer? And where is Little Fawn?"

"In the village. I had been in the woods and came back and found White Feather with pain. I had taken Little Fawn to the village to stay with Sunflower and to fetch the medicine woman to come and help White Feather with the birth." He smiled at his friend. "I guess we won't need her now."

"No," chuckled Tsu-la.

"We have a son, Tsu-la." He smiled, and turned to gaze at his friend. Suddenly, he realized why Tsu-la had come and his words of elation halted. "Tsu-la, have you not changed your mind about leaving tomorrow?"

"No," Tsu-la answered, "I am going. There are others from our village leaving also. Please come with us...when White Feather can travel again."

"No, my friend, we will stay. White Feather will never leave."

"You know that you will be forced to leave someday," Tsu-la said.

"Perhaps," Running Deer answered. "Perhaps not. White Feather could never be happy anywhere except here in the mountains."

Both of the men grew silent, and stared at the tall green forest in front of them. The sun would soon drop behind the hills and night would come, bringing its darkness and cool crisp air.

Sometime later, Tsu-la interrupted their quiet meditation as he rose. "I will speak to White Feather now," he said softly.

When Tsu-la entered the cabin, the sleeping mother awoke. Seeing his face, she now knew that this was the time she had long dreaded. Tsu-la knelt beside the bed and placed his hand on the sleeping child. Then, he stood and walked to the door, stopped and looked back. "I will see you again, White Feather," he said, and then was gone.

"No," she whispered softly, but Tsu-la did not hear.

The two men stood on the porch. Tsu-la spoke, "I will see you again, my friend. You know that, don't you?"

Running Deer said nothing.

Tsu-la placed his hand on the shoulder of his friend; Running Deer's hand rose to Tsu-la's shoulder and the two solemnly gazed into the depth of their friendship.

"We are of the same Longhair Clan. I will be with you again," Tsu-la said, then turned and walked away, leaving Running Deer to watch his friend walk out of his life. When he reached the trail, Tsu-la looked back and Running Deer raised his hand in a final parting gesture.

"I will miss you, Tsu-la," Running Deer whispered as he watched him disappear around the bend in the trail.

CHAPTER THIRTEEN

Gv-nv-ge Yo-na

Careful not to disturb White Feather, Running Deer lifted a small stool and carried it across the room to sit close to his wife's bedside.

"Much has happened today," he mused as he sat quietly.

In the silence of the room, he reflected on his adventure in the woods earlier in the day. The mission of his trip had been accomplished, he thought with satisfaction. The true meaning of his absence had not been to hunt for game, as he had told White Feather, but to search for something different, and gratefully, he had found what he needed. It troubled Running Deer to know that he had deceived his wife and pangs of guilt swept over him when he thought of the deception. He could not share his findings with White Feather. But she would understand someday when he would tell her the truth, when the time arrived and indicated that she should know of his mission. But, for now, he must hold the secret deep in his heart.

His mind wandered. He had glimpsed the unhap-

py group of his Cherokee friends who had gathered by
the church to make final plans for their departure
when he was in the village earlier in the day. In his
haste to return to White Feather, Running Deer regret-
fully remembered that he had not stopped to bid them
farewell. It saddened him to know that he would
never see these friends again. He had managed a brief
wave in their direction as he ran though the village
and received a few nods from the people. Most of the
group sat motionless, heads bowed, their meager
belongings gathered around their feet in preparation
for the long trip ahead of them. Running Deer wondered if they would survive the trip to the west. They
chose to go, he reminded himself. "Perhaps they will
find happiness in their new homeland," he thought.

     Tsu-la...gone forever from his life now. He
would miss him.

     White Feather moved slightly and Running Deer
leaned quickly toward her. "Look at our son, Running
Deer. Is he not handsome?" she smiled sleepily,
uncovering the infant for Running Deer to view the
chubby little body.

     "Yes," he answered as he touched the child's
hand. The infant's fingers closed and tightened
around Running Deer's thumb.

     Running Deer smiled. "He is strong." He
stroked the mass of long hair on the baby's head.

     "He has thick black hair," Running Deer
remarked, "the hair of a Gv-nv-ge Yo-na (Black Bear),"
he smiled, stroking the baby's hair again.
"Hummm...Gv-nv-ge Yo-na," Running Deer said slowly. "He will be called Gv-nv-ge Yo-na. Do you not
agree?" he asked, looking quickly at his wife.

     "Yes," approved White Feather. "Gv-nv-ge Yo-
na...a good name for him, my husband," she laughed.

     Running Deer wrapped the covering around the
baby and carefully lifted the child into his strong
arms. He walked to the porch and looked out at the
peaceful valley surrounding the cabin, now bathed in
soft moonlight.

     "Look O-sti (little one)," he said elevating the

baby's head and turning Gv-nv-ge Yo-na toward the mountains, " Here in the land of your Cherokee ancestors is where you were born." He gazed at the serene beauty around him. And smiling, forgetting the present turmoil surrounding his people, Running Deer thought of all the things he would teach his son here in the mountains. He and Gv-nv-ge Yo-na would hunt and fish together, swim in the river and plant seeds for food and care for the land. Gv-nv-ge Yo-na would grow to love his home as his ancestors did.

He frowned, saying aloud, "So much lies ahead for you, Gv-nv-ge Yo-na, as you grow into manhood. You must stand tall in the changing world you are entering. You must be strong to meet the difficulties that lie ahead. You must grow in strength that will help you face the dangers of life. Gv-nv-ge Yo-na, you must be strong to meet your fate, whatever it may be." The man gazed intently into the child's face as he continued, "Your father, Running Deer, will teach you these things. He will teach Gv-nv-ge Yo-na to love the Cherokee country of his people. You, Gv-nv-ge Yo-na, will grow up loving all mankind with peace in your heart."

Gv-nv-ge Yo-na responded to his father's speech with loud wails. Smiling, Running Deer pulled the child close to his chest and went back inside the cabin.

"Gv-nv-ge Yo-na is back. He wants his mother," he laughed, laying the child close to White Feather on the bed.

"Can you eat, White Feather? Are you hungry?" he asked, lighting a lamp to brighten the room.

"Yes, I am as hungry as Gv-nv-ge Yo-na seems to be," she laughed lightly watching the infant eagerly nursing her breast.

"I will give you food and then go to get Little Fawn. I want her to meet her new brother."

CHAPTER FOURTEEN

Going to the Water

Tsu-la had not slept well. He slowly opened his eyes, adjusting them to the darkness of the room around him. He had lain awake much of the night in anticipation of the coming day that would change his life.

He rose from his bunk and lit a small candle to cast light into the room. He must hurry now. The soldiers would probably arrive in the village soon.

He quickly dressed. In the dimness of the candlelight he moved about in the room, gathering his few belongings. He placed them neatly in a pile by the door, ready to be retrieved when the soldiers came.

In the dawning light, now brightening the room, Tsu-la stood in the center of the small cabin and paused. He had been happy here, when Morning Star had been by his side.

He moved slowly to the burning candle and blew out the flame. He stood and watched as the smoke rose and disappeared into the room. For a moment he did not move.

Sighing, he then walked to the door and eased it

open. He stepped outside and cast his gaze toward the village. He saw no one. He walked away from the cabin, directing his feet toward the path leading to the river. He would go to the water once more.

Suddenly the sun burst from behind the mountains, casting its bright warm rays through the cloudy mist draped over the settlement.

"A new day begins," he said thoughtfully. "The old days are gone."

He reached the river and stood on its sloping bank. Quickly shedding his clothes and moccasins, he waded into the icy water. He wanted to revitalize his spirit and strength, so in Cherokee tradition, he prayed and ritually dunked himself in the water seven times.

In the quiet thereafter, Tsu-la silently vowed that he would never forget the feel of this river on his body nor the beauty of its presence. The river would remain buried close to his heart forever. He closed his eyes and meditated.

Suddenly, there was the clatter of hooves. Horses were approaching on the road leading into the village.

"The soldiers," he thought, and his eyes sprang open. "The soldiers have come early."

He climbed from the water and hurriedly pulled his clothes on over his wet body. Today there was not time to lie in the sun to dry himself before dressing. He must hurry.

Slipping his moccasins onto his feet, he ran quickly toward the village. He did not want to be left behind.

He slowed his pace as he neared the settlement and saw the small company of soldiers dismounting their horses near the church and heard one soldier shouting orders to the people.

The Cherokee who would leave today were moving slowly toward the Army men, carrying their few possessions in their arms or on their backs.

Tsu-la could hear the soft mournful cries of the refugees' friends who were following close behind them. He was glad that he had said his goodbyes yesterday. He did not want them to see his sadness when he walked out of the village for the last time.

He rushed into his cabin and quickly gathered the belongings he had left by the door. Casting a final glance at his home he hurried away to join the soldiers.

CHAPTER FIFTEEN

May 23, 1838

May 23, 1838 dawned to a cloudless blue sky. Midmorning sun softly touched White Feather while she sat on the cabin's lowest step watching her children playing in the yard nearby.

White Feather gathered the skirt of her long calico dress into her hands and pulled it up to her knees, then quickly leaned down and slipped off her soft deerskin moccasins and laid them aside. She loved the feel of the land beneath her feet and she gently caressed the warm earth with her bare toes.

"Soon the hot days will come," she thought with a smile, eagerly anticipating the summer months ahead when she could go without her moccasins.

With a peaceful sigh, White Feather placed her elbows on the upper step behind her and leaned back on them. She closed her eyes and tilted her head back, allowing the sun to embrace her face.

In the distance, she heard the familiar chirping of birds and the rush of the river. White Feather and the children were alone. She longed for Running Deer to be sitting beside her to enjoy the day with her.

Running Deer had completed his morning work on the little farm early and had left his wife and children to go down river.

"We will have fresh fish to eat tonight," he had promised with a smile when he left the cabin.

When he reached the river's edge he turned and waved to them, then disappeared, moving downstream toward the traps in the river's deepest water.

It was rare times now when Running Deer left White Feather and the children alone at the cabin. Each day Running Deer's dark eyes kept a constant vigil for the white soldier's return to their quiet homeland. He knew that the soldiers would suddenly appear one day and he feared for the safety of his family.

White Feather's quiet reverie was suddenly interrupted by peals of laughter from Little Fawn and Gv-nv-ge Yo-na. She opened her eyes to gaze at her children engaged in their childhood play.

Little Fawn squealed in delight as she teased her good-natured little brother who stood looking at her. She tapped Gv-nv-ge Yo-na lightly on the shoulder, ran a few steps away from him, paused and encouraged him to run and catch her.

Gv-nv-ge Yo-na's young legs carried him unsteadily toward Little Fawn, but after a few steps, he fell upon the soft grass, unhurt. He laughed and rolled over, placed his hands firmly on the ground and pushed himself to a standing position. Little Fawn beckoned him to come to her again and Gv-nv-ge Yo-na tottered toward his sister once more, only to trip and fall again

White Feather smiled at Gv-nv-ge Yo-na, amused at the child's determination to reach his sister's side.

"Poor little Gv-nv-ge Yo-na. Your legs are not yet fast enough to keep up with your sister," White Feather offered sympathetically to her younger child. "Soon they will become stronger and you will run faster."

Watching the childish antics of her little ones,

White Feather thought of how much she loved them.
"They are happy children," White Feather thought.
"They are strong and healthy...and growing taller each
day. Soon Gv-nv-ge Yo-na will go to the river with
Running Deer."

Little Fawn waited patiently for Gv-nv-ge Yo-na
to rise and reach her, then turned and ran away,
laughing as Gv-nv-ge Yo-na slowly came toward her.

The children were always eager to learn new
things. Their parents enjoyed teaching them the ways
of their ancestors and the appreciation for the
Cherokee lands around them.

Little Fawn, who had the delicate facial features
of her mother, possessed quickness for learning and
White Feather had begun teaching the child the art of
basket weaving while they sat indoors by the fireplace
during the long winter months. Little Fawn's hands
moved clumsily at the task, but her awkwardness did
not quench the child's desire to learn to weave beautiful baskets like the ones her mother made. She spent
long periods of time at her mother's side, patiently following instructions, never tiring from her attempts to
learn to weave. She had listened with interest when
White Feather spoke to her of going into the woods for
the bark of the black walnut tree to make the dye for
the white oak baskets. "Little Fawn will someday be a
very fine basket weaver," White Feather had thought
as she watched the child's determined progress in
learning to weave.

White Feather's gaze took in Gv-nv-ge Yo-na as
he moved about in front of her. He resembled his
father so strongly that it was a constant source of
amazement to White Feather each time she looked
into the child's face. Gv-nv-ge Yo-na, a tall child for a
year old, had walked at only eight months, his ener-
getic body moved about constantly, investigating
everything within the reach of his hands. Often his
mischievousness had gotten him into trouble as he
eagerly explored his surroundings.

All at once, White Feather's thoughts turned to
Tsu-la. He had never heard the name Running Deer

had given their child. She wished he were back living in the village again. She wished that he could see the children playing together today. She missed her friend. He had left the village a year ago and no one had heard anything from him since his departure.

"I wonder where he lives today," she mused, looking up at the vast blue sky. "I hope he is happy, wherever he is...in the west."

She had thought often about the soldiers returning after Tsu-la left with them. They knew where the settlement was located and this bothered White Feather. For weeks she had slept lightly, waking often, her ears alert for the sounds that could be the military men approaching her home. The days of anxiety had progressed into months and White Feather watched daily for the soldiers' return, ready to take her children and run to hide in the high mountains until their search was over. She was sure that Running Deer would go with her and the children but he never responded when she talked of her plan to elude the soldiers.

Time had passed and there had been no sign of the military men. White Feather had begun to relax. She was now sure that they had forgotten about the Cherokee in their small secluded settlement. Hopefully, she had also thought that perhaps John Ross had been successful in gaining a reprieve for the Indians so they would be allowed to remain in their homeland. She and Running Deer had continued their lives in peace without interruption from the white government and she had enthusiastically helped plant the garden that would provide food in the coming months.

When the warm days of spring approached Running Deer had taken his family to the village several times to visit their friends that they had missed seeing during the long snowy winter days when travel was impossible. White Feather had observed that the village people had continued their lives in peace also, assured that the soldiers would not return to evict them from their homes.

White Feather sat up, straightened her body and stretched her arms. She sighed with a smile of contentment. She turned her eyes upward toward the quiet mountains in the distance. Her heart was filled with peacefulness, thinking that at last her life would be left undisturbed by the wrath of the white government.

Just over the horizon, clouds formed, ringing the land with shadows.

CHAPTER SIXTEEN

Dark Cloud of Cruelty

White Feather's children had grown tired of playing together and now Little Fawn sat on the grass entertaining herself with the wooden bear Running Deer had carved for her. Gv-nv-ge Yo-na sat near his sister on the ground, softly fretting, irritable from the weariness in his legs.

Reluctantly White Feather slipped her soft moccasins onto her bare feet and stood.

"Gv-nv-ge Yo-na is tired, he needs rest," she thought, walking to the young child and lifting him into her arms. "Come, Gv-nv-ge Yo-na," she soothed, hugging the small body closely, "you must rest for a while."

Gv-nv-ge Yo-na laid his head on White Feather's shoulder and relaxed, welcoming his mother's arms and comforted by the closeness of her body.

White Feather climbed the cabin's steps and paused when she reached the open door of the cabin, turning to look at Little Fawn. Just beyond the tops of the trees, an unusual dark cloud hung low in the sky, hovering over the land in the direction of the village.

"That is strange," she thought. "I have not seen this cloud before."

She dismissed her suspicions, remembering that a spring rain in the mountains could come quickly.

"Little Fawn, play near," she said, motioning toward the steps. "Play here." She turned to enter the cabin, then stopped at the sound of a low rumbling. She paused to listen more carefully, but heard nothing.

"My ears are playing tricks on me today," she smiled, moving to the inside of the cabin.

She laid Gv-nv-ge Yo-na on his bunk and sat beside him, stroking his long black silky hair. "Sleep, little Gv-nv-ge Yo-na," she cooed lovingly to the child. Exhausted, he settled into sleep.

White Feather kissed his face, then rose and walked to the door.

Seeing that Little Fawn had moved from the yard and now sat on the bottom step playing with the bear, White Feather was satisfied. She glanced upward again at the dark cloud which was now rapidly approaching the cabin. She wished that Running Deer would return before the rain.

"If the rain comes, Little Fawn, hurry inside," she told the child.

"Soon the spring rain will bring water to our garden. That is good," she mused as she turned to go inside the cabin.

She walked to the fireplace and began preparing cornbread to go with the squirrel stew that was simmering in the large iron pot hung over the fire in the fireplace. She knew that Running Deer would be hungry when he returned from inspecting the fish traps and would want to eat before he began cleaning the fish.

Suddenly her thoughts of Running Deer were interrupted. A long piercing scream echoed through the room, startling White Feather and causing her to drop the dish she held in her hands. She ran quickly to the open door, almost tripping in her haste to follow the frightened cries of Little Fawn. She froze in her tracks when she reached the porch. Her heart beat wildly for her gaze met soldiers, six in number, mounted on horses, except for one horse with no rider. The men in blue coats stared at her. Her attention fell on the vacant step where Little Fawn had sat moments before and her heart beat rapidly in terror. The sound of the child's crying was now in the distance. Horrified, she saw a soldier running away from the cabin toward the woods with the struggling child in his arms.

"Little Fawn!" White Feather screamed and ran after the child, who was disappearing into the woods.

The frantic mother ran toward the thick trees, but strong hands abruptly grabbed her harshly. The man pulled White Feather around quickly and into his arms, pinning her against his chest. She screamed the child's name again and struggled. Blinded by her tears she kicked wildly at her captor, swinging each leg with all her strength. He stepped back to avoid her attack, laughing, and White Feather freed one hand and raked her fingernails down the side of his face, leaving a long thin red line of blood. Her strength, no match for the bruising hands of the soldier, waned as he caught her free hand and pinned both of her arms behind her back.

"Well, now, you're a real little spit-fire, ain't you?" her captor leered into her face.

She felt sickened by his foul-smelling breath. He turned his head briefly to spit tobacco juice on the ground near her feet.

"I bet a little squaw like you can show a man a lot of fun," he laughed, pulling her close against him.

With regained strength White Feather fought wildly in an attempt to free herself. When the soldier leaned his head back to laugh again, she jerked her arms loose and attempted to run, but he grabbed her shoulder, spun her around and pushed her to the ground. She rose and again tried to run, but the laughing soldier trapped her and pulled her back into his arms. "Come'er squaw!"

"Little Fawn! Little Fawn!" she cried, her anguished gaze searching the woods where her child had disappeared with the soldier.

"Leave her alone, Benson," a stern voice spoke from behind White Feather.

"She likes it!" her captor snarled.

"Leave her be," the now commanding voice spoke again. White Feather turned her head and saw a tall light-haired soldier who looked to be no older than she.

"Shut up, Levi," White Feather's captor replied, turning to look scornfully at the compassionate soldier. "I'm just having myself a little fun," he jeered. "She shore is a pretty thing...for a squaw, that is!" he laughed into White Feather's face.

White Feather struggled to free herself once again. Her movements halted suddenly at the sound of a familiar voice calling her name in the distance. "Running Deer," she thought, relieved that he had returned. "Running Deer," she whispered.

She turned her head and saw Running Deer coming toward them from the woods by the river. His face dark with anger,White Feather saw him drop the fish and draw his knife.

The soldiers swiftly dismounted from their horses and stood waiting with drawn rifles.

As he ran by the group of men, one of the soldiers held his rifle in both hands, and struck Running Deer on the head with the butt end, sending him face first into the ground.

White Feather screamed.

Running Deer's attempts to rise failed, just as another soldier stepped forward and quickly seized the knife from his hand, planting his foot heavily on his back.

"Stinking injun!" the soldier spat, and kicked him under the chin.

White Feather screamed again and freed herself. Quickly she ran to Running Deer and fell on her knees beside her husband, pulling him into her arms.

The young Indian man sat up slowly, removed

the turban from his head and used it to wipe the blood from the gaping gash on his chin.

"Running Deer...." White Feather sobbed, wiping the blood away with her hand.

"I am all right," Running Deer said quietly. "Have they hurt you?" he asked.

"No...but Little Fawn...they have taken Little Fawn," stammered White Feather.

"Little Fawn?"

"Yes...a soldier...stole her and ran away with her...."

Running Deer's anger rose to a new pitch and he struggled to rise, but received another blow to the back of his head from a soldier looming over him.

He lunged forward, falling face-first on the ground.

White Feather slipped her arms around her husband, shielding him close to her body. A soldier's foot stepped into her eyesight.

"Now get up and go inside that cabin and get what you can carry! Make it quick!"

"Yeah! Get up!" Benson added, kicking Running Deer in the back. "We ain't got...!"

The command was suddenly interrupted by the sound of a horse approaching.

"It's the captain," a soldier whispered as the rider came into view. The Indian couple saw the soldiers quickly move away from them.

"What's going on here, Sergeant?" The rider halted his horse in front of the soldiers.

"These Injuns were giving us trouble, Captain." Benson replied.

"Trouble?"

"Yes, Sir!"

"What kind of trouble?"

"They refused to come to the stockade with us, Sir," Benson lied.

White Feather turned an incredible gaze toward Benson, noting that his eyes avoided looking at her and Running Deer.

"That is not true," she said hoarsely, looking at

the officer and then was momentarily startled at the recognition of the military man.

"It's the captain...." she thought unbelievingly, "The captain who came to our village meeting."

White Feather and the captain's eyes met briefly.

The captain frowned at the sight of the fresh blood on Running Deer's head. "Who wounded this man?"

"I did, Sir. He had a knife."

"I'll speak to you later, soldier," the captain promised.

"But, Sir, he...."

"I said, I'll speak to you later," the captain repeated angrily.

"Yes, Sir!" the soldier answered, taking a step backward.

"Now, leave these people alone," the captain warned strongly. "Do you understand?"

"Yes, Sir," the soldiers responded, one by one.

The captain paused, regained his composure and then turned to White Feather and Running Deer, addressing them kindly.

"Go. Get your belongings. We must leave as soon as possible."

The captain's gaze never left the Indian couple as he watched them rise slowly to their feet, their arms locked together, supporting each other.

White Feather straightened, looking tearfully at the captain. She took a step toward him and he saw the now darkening bruises on White Feather's swollen wrists and arms. New anger swelled up in the captain. The soldier would be punished, he promised himself.

"A soldier has stolen Little Fawn from us," she began. Her voice broke.

"Little Fawn?"

"Our child," Running Deer answered.

The captain turned to face the soldiers. "Where is the child of these people?"

Before any of them could answer all eyes turned

to the village path where a soldier was returning on foot, hurrying toward the group.

White Feather gasped in terror. Little Fawn was not with him.

"Soldier! Get over here!" the captain ordered sharply. "Where is the child?"

"She is in the village with the other Cherokees, Sir."

"Why did you take the child?"

"I thought her parents would come peacefully, Sir, if I took their child first, Sir."

The captain turned away from him, his deep anger controlled.

"She is safe with your people," he assured the couple. "Now, go. Get your belongings. We must hurry."

The captain then turned his horse toward the village path and rode slowly away. As he passed the soldiers he cast a stern look in their direction

The Cherokee couple and the soldiers silently watched as the captain disappeared down the trail. No one moved until he was well out of earshot.

"The captain's going soft in the head about these Indians," Benson muttered to himself as he walked away from White Feather and Running Deer.

The young soldier who had attempted to halt Benson stepped forward.

"Go to your cabin. We will wait for you to get your things, but you must hurry," he said. "We must leave soon."

"Leave?" thought White Feather. "This is my home."

CHAPTER SEVENTEEN

Exhausted Reflection

Exhaustion overtook Captain Howard. His eyes burned and the lump in his throat ached at remembering White Feather and Running Deer sitting on the ground surrounded by strange men holding rifles aimed at them. Their faces, filled with hurt and anguish from the treatment they had received from the soldiers, taunted the captain's thoughts while he rode slowly back to the village.

"It's unnecessary to treat the Cherokee cruelly," he thought. "The soldier who struck Running Deer will be dealt with...I will see to it."

Like many of the local white people, Captain Howard's heart ached for the Cherokee whose tears he had witnessed during the past few days during his leadership in the final roundup of the Indians in Georgia.

Following the meeting in the Cherokee village over a year ago, Captain Howard had remained stationed at Fort Wool awaiting orders for his next assignment. When the captain had first arrived at the fort he had watched as soldiers began cutting trees and building the stockade near the fort. "This is only an animal corral!" Captain Howard had thought. It was not fit for humans. He watched daily until the stockade was completed. He had prayed that the Indians would not be held in captivity for a long period of time because he did not think they could survive the conditions...no covering, no place to sit except on the ground, and no sanitary provisions; only timbers forming a fence enclosing the area. Captain Howard could not believe that people would be placed in the enclosure. It was inhuman.

Days had passed. No word had been received concerning his involvement in the Indian removal so he grew hopeful. Maybe he would be spared from the grueling task of evicting the Indians from their homes. And then the colonel called him to his quarters and read him his assignment. He would oversee the arrival of the Cherokee who were being brought to the stockade. A wave of sickness ran through his body each time a new group of proud Cherokee arrived at the stockade prison.

After a few weeks, the captain received additional orders.He was to search every remote cabin hidden away in the Cherokee lands, bringing the Indians to the stockade as quickly as possible by whatever means it took. The two years were about up.

The captain had been riding and searching for days with little rest. The days had been long and tiresome, his body exhausted from emotional strain.

Riding through the green forest he could understand why the Indians would never agree to leave. The beauty of this spot in the Cherokee lands overwhelmed him. He vowed he would return someday when this miscarriage of justice was over.

The village came into view and his thoughts of the Indian family ceased. Coming closer to the village he sighed, filling his lungs deeply with the fresh mountain air and he straightened himself in the saddle. He pulled his shoulders upright.

Riding slowly into the settlement his gaze fell on

an old Cherokee woman sitting on the ground, her back supported by the trunk of a large oak tree. In her lap she held a frightened girl whom she was attempting to console. Looking closely, he recognized the child. Little Fawn, her parents had called her. He rode on slowly past the old woman and the child, his gaze resting on them until they were behind him. As soon as the child's parents were brought in to join the others they would be required to march the people into the prison and lock the gates to await removal from their homeland.

The captain closed his eyes and shuddered.

CHAPTER EIGHTEEN

Bundle of Belongings

White Feather did not move. Numb with shock, she refused to believe what was happening. Her dark eyes narrowed as she watched the young private turn and walk toward the cabin. The soldier sat on the top step and laid his rifle across his bent knees. He motioned for them to come to the cabin.

"Go away!" White Feather thought. She trembled.

Running Deer's arms tightened. "White Feather," he whispered softly, "we must go with the soldiers."

"No!" she cried.

"Yes."

"No!" she repeated. "Go to the village and bring Little Fawn back to us. Then we will run and hide in the mountains."

"It is not possible now, White Feather. It is too late," he said, glancing around at the soldiers surrounding them.

"Yes!" she insisted.

"No, White Feather. It is not possible," he responded, as he wiped away the trickle of blood oozing from his wound.

"Yes! We will run into the woods," she whispered glancing over her shoulder at the soldiers. "They will not find us in the high mountains."

A frightened wail split the air. Gv-nv-ge Yo-na stood in the doorway of the cabin. The sight of the blue-coated strangers prompted his crying to become louder and more frantic as his gaze scanned the yard for White Feather.

The relaxing soldiers' conversations halted unexpectedly at the sound of a child's crying and they turned curious stares toward Gv-nv-ge Yo-na.

"Well, looka there!" a soldier's voice sneered. "There's another one of them stinking Injuns we got to drag to the stockade with us."

"Yeah...reckon he's got a knife too?" Benson laughed.

Running Deer's body stiffened. He dropped his arms to his sides and clenched his hands into fists in anger. Glaring at the sergeant, Running Deer fought for control against the rising rage surfacing within his body. His dark eyes flared.

"Running Deer...." White Feather whispered, alarmed. She placed her hands on his broad chest and stepped in front of him, halting him before he started "No!" she warned.

Benson laughed again, turning his back to Running Deer as he spoke low to the soldiers around him who laughed also.

Gv-nv-ge Yo-na's crying became louder and more frantic and the couple looked back at their child. Blinded by his tears Gv-nv-ge Yo-na's uncertain steps had carried him dangerously close to the edge of the open porch.

White Feather caught her breath in terror fearing that the child would fall.

"Go to Gv-nv-ge Yo-na," Running Deer's ragged voice told White Feather. "Go to him. I will get our cow from the barn. We will need milk on the journey."

White Feather pushed the private aside as she ran up the steps to reach her child. She lifted Gv-nv-ge Yo-na into her arms and cradled him, then began rocking him gently.

Her clouded eyes swept across the yard watching Running Deer as he made his way slowly toward the barn. A soldier followed, his rifle at Running Deer's back.

The young private on the porch motioned for White Feather to move inside the cabin.

She turned and walked slowly toward the door. Heavy footsteps behind her alerted her to the presence of Sergeant Benson.

"Get a move on, squaw," he ordered harshly.

Gv-nv-ge Yo-na, frightened, began crying again.

"Shut up!" Benson bellowed and stood for a moment in the center of the cabin, his gaze exploring its interior.

For a second, White Feather held her son close, soothing him. Then, placing him on the floor, she pulled a blanket from the bunk and spread it open on the floor. She moved slowly about the room in a daze, gathering clothes for the family and laying them in the middle of the blanket.

Suddenly Gv-nv-ge Yo-na's whimpering stopped and White Feather glanced around quickly, frightened that he too, could have been kidnapped.

Stooping down beside Gv-nv-ge Yo-na, the young private was speaking gently to the little boy, quieting him.

White Feather hurried to her child, ready to pull him into her arms, but the private smiled at White Feather. His kind eyes told White Feather that he would not bring harm to the child. Still, she did not trust the white soldier with the rifle. Reluctantly, she moved away, keeping a watchful eye on Gv-nv-ge Yo-na.

She added a bearskin to the pile of clothes on the blanket and turned, nearly loosing her footing when Benson pushed past her to ramble about in the room. He plundered through the family's possessions in the cabin, searching for something of value.

"These Injuns ain't got nothing," he muttered, overturning a basket and noisily throwing things onto the floor.

He pillaged his way through the room, finally stopping at the table where a plate had been set for Running Deer. The sergeant's beefy hand reached down to pick up a large piece of cold cornbread from the table and he stuffed it greedily into his mouth. His beady eyes focused on the wall above the fireplace.

"What's that?" he questioned through a mouthful of food. He squinted his eyes and moved closer to the fireplace.

On a small wooden peg hung White Feather's beaded wedding necklace.

White Feather had spent many days stringing the small colorful beads to create the intricate designs in the necklace; she had worn it with pride on her wedding day.

White Feather froze. He had discovered her necklace. Quickly, he stuffed her precious wedding necklace deep into his coat pocket.

Benson looked at the private and laughed, satisfied at finding something of interest to steal.

"My wife will like this little trinket," he grinned, patting his pocket.

"Sir, begging your pardon, Sir, the Captain will not like what you are doing," the young private ventured bravely to his superior.

"Well, he ain't got to know, now does he?" Benson tossed back over his shoulder, resuming his plundering through the room.

The private spoke again, "The Captain ordered that we do not steal from the Cherokee, Sir."

Benson turned quickly to glare at the grieving White Feather and the private standing beside her. "Ain't nobody gonna tell 'em, now are they?" He pointed his rifle at the pair. "And if they do...click!"

He howled a raucous laugh and began his plundering once again while White Feather watched him, inflamed by his words. "There is no good in him."

She thought, staring with contempt in her eyes.

Benson felt White Feather's gaze. He turned his head and leered back over his shoulder. "Hurry up, squaw. Get a move on!"

White Feather leaned down and pulled the corners of the outspread blanket together, attempting to pull it up from the floor, but its weight was too heavy for her to lift. Discouraged, she opened the bundle and cast aside all of its contents except for one blanket and a few clothes. She knotted the corners of the blanket together. From a peg on the wall, she gathered another blanket to throw open on the floor. To this she added another blanket and then walked to the fireplace to retrieve a cooking vessel from the hearth. She placed the remaining cornbread in it and put the pot on the outspread blanket, thinking that the children would be hungry soon. Her hands moved quickly to knot the corners of this blanket together. She scanned the simmering stew over the fire, wishing the soldiers would allow them the time to eat before they left, but she knew that it would be impossible.

Benson approached her from behind and pushed the hard rifle into her back.

"Get your little Injun and let's go. We ain't got all day," he ordered roughly, bored now that he found nothing else to steal from the cabin.

White Feather picked up the smaller bundle containing the food and put her arm through the opening below the knotted ends, pushing the blanket to her back. She lifted Gv-nv-ge Yo-na and held him in one arm while stretching to lift the remaining bundle from the floor. But, the young private reached out and picked it up.

"Now you're fetching and carrying for these stinking Injuns," Benson sneered when he saw the private pick up the blanket. "I think you're going soft in the head, Private."

"It doesn't hurt to offer a little kindness to anyone," the private spoke softly, more to himself than to the sergeant.

Benson neared White Feather and prodded her

again in the back with his rifle, pushing her through the doorway and out onto the porch. The private followed. As she went out the door, White Feather saw the the old spinning wheel that had belonged to her mother. It represented the old ways. When her mother died, White Feather had inherited it. Someday it was to belong to Little Fawn.

She walked through the door. The dark cloud now hung over the little cabin. White Feather looked at the distant hazy mountains and listened to the sound of the gentle river rushing over the rocks. This was her home, and the familiar sights and sounds embraced her heart. A sharpness stabbed her back, almost causing her to lose her footing as she stumbled down the steps.

On the ground, half-hidden by a tall bush was Little Fawn's discarded wooden bear. She stooped, her fingers closing around the bear, concealing it from the sergeant's eyes.

"Get along, squaw," Benson bellowed.

Clutching the bear tightly in her hand, White Feather straightened and adjusted the load on her back, smiling slightly with satisfaction.

"I said – MOVE!" the cruel voice yelled behind her, pushing her again. Looking ahead White Feather saw Running Deer and the soldier returning from the barn without the cow. She ran to her husband followed by the private clutching her bundle of belongings.

Running Deer took Gv-nv-ge Yo-na from White Feather's arms. He looked at the kind soldier who handed him the blanket bundle. He nodded, thanking the soldier for his kindness.

"The cow? Where is our cow?" said White Feather to her husband.

"The cow is gone."

"Gone?"

"Yes. One of the soldiers took it away while you were in the cabin."

"No!" White Feather cried. "The cow belongs to us. The children will need milk…they…."

"The soldiers say that it will be needed for food," Running Deer answered quietly.

White Feather stared at Running Deer, then shifted her eyes to the mountains. "Maybe, maybe we can run into the mountains now," she thought.

"Let's go.... Move!" Benson demanded roughly as he approached the couple and their child. We've got to get out of here." He quickly mounted his waiting horse and led the detail of soldiers toward the Indian couple.

At the bend in the trail White Feather hesitated, turning to gaze back at her home. Her hands flew to her mouth, and she screamed. Black smoke belched out of the windows and door as the flames ate their way through the cabin.

Grief filled her chest as she watched the flames burst through the roof. She thought of the old spinning wheel, the rough-cut table, the stew on the fire. She hung her head. The cabin they had worked so hard to build, the garden now ready for reaping, the fence rails Running Deer had laboriously split, the barn, the flowers in the yard...all were gone or trampled or broken. Through misted eyes she looked upward toward the silent mountains and whispered, "I will come back. I will return to the land of my people someday."

White Feather could feel the breath of the horses against her back as they nudged her forward. She stumbled down the trail.

Behind her, quick flames licked the chimney, spitting dark clouds into the sky. Thunder sounded beyond the mountain ridges and into it's depth walked despair.

CHAPTER NINETEEN

The Stockade

White Feather's feet hurt and her legs burned with throbbing pains that shot upward from the bottoms of her thin moccasins. She ran her hand across her aching brow, sighing deeply.

The Cherokee had been walking for hours and they were all exhausted from the tiring trek. She wondered if they would ever reach a place where the soldiers would allow them to stop and rest. She had no idea where they were; the surroundings had become unfamiliar to her after they passed through the New Echota area of Georgia. Years ago she had visited the Cherokee capital, but she had never gone north of the town, so the land looked new and different.

Gv-nv-ge Yo-na, tired and hungry, fretted in White Feather's arms. She shifted him to the other hip and rubbed his back, in an attempt to soothe the little boy. She had been carrying her child a long time and her back ached from fatigue.

Running Deer, arms loaded with the bundles they had brought from home, had told Little Fawn to hold onto his breeches as she walked beside him.

Every once in a while, the parents would switch duties, but Running Deer would often carry both of his children at the same time.

The walk had exhausted the children, and White Feather wished she could stop and feed them or at least let them take a nap. If the caravan of Indians attempted to pause the soldiers' horses following close behind would push them forward again.

White Feather turned slightly and glanced behind, her gaze resting briefly on the wagon following. The elders of the village who were unable to walk long distances had been put in wagons to ride with the Cherokee who were too sick to walk.

"Poor Moon Face," White Feather thought sadly, knowing that the old woman was in one of the wagons.

Moon Face had begged to be left behind, but it was not allowed. Before they left the village Moon Face had finally resigned herself to her fate. Falling on her knees outside her cabin door, she prayed in Cherokee while the astonished soldiers stood by and silently watched. Then the aged woman arose, her face wet with tears of sorrow. She was gently helped into one of the wagons by a compassionate soldier.

"Perhaps," White Feather thought hopefully, "her health will improve with the anticipation of seeing Tsu-la again...if she endures the long trip."

Abruptly the Cherokee procession stopped in a clearing in the woods and White Feather strained to see what had occurred at the front of the line. Standing on tiptoes she looked up over the heads of those in front of her. She saw what appeared to be a wooden building.

"Running Deer," she whispered, "what is happening?"

Her husband's face was grim and he stared straight ahead in disbelief.

"Running Deer?"

He shook his head slowly and did not answer. He continued to stare ahead toward the structure.

Loud shouting penetrated the air. White Feather could not make out nor understand the words. She strained to listen. When the voice rang out again, the only words she could hear were, "Open the gate."

She was bewildered. The procession began moving again and White Feather pressed close to Running Deer.

When they neared the building White Feather stopped and stared at it, aghast. Looming before them was the structure that she had thought was a building, but on closer inspection she realized that it looked more like a large animal pen with four tall wooden sides. Clearly perplexed, she could not see the roof of the building. Both large gates facing the Cherokee had been swung open and the Indians were filing into the stockade. Soldiers standing at the gates were pushing the refugees to enter, motioning with the bayonets on the ends of their rifles.

White Feather, with Running Deer and their children, moved through the gates and reluctantly entered the enclosure. The gates slammed shut! No longer unsure of what was happening, White Feather now knew this would be their prison until they continued their journey to the west.

Suddenly White Feather espied Moon Face in the crowd. The old woman had climbed out of the wagon and was struggling to walk toward the gates when a soldier moved to her side and waved his rifle threateningly at her.

Intending to fend off the soldier, White Feather ran to the elderly woman's side and put a protective arm around her. The old woman, trembling with weakness and fatigue, leaned against her protector.

"Come," White Feather said softly, "come with me." She led Moon Face to Running Deer and the children. "We will take care of you."

"Yes," said Running Deer, "you will stay with us. We will care for you."

The Indians stood huddled together in the middle of the stockade, dazed. Soft weeping from some of the Cherokee women swept the grassy earth, while

loud wails erupted from the frightened, hungry children. Silent pain rising from suffering souls stabbed
into the twilight of evening.

CHAPTER TWENTY

The Unconquerable Spirit

Days passed; long torturous days. The Cherokee remained locked in the stockade. Bewildered, they hovered in groups within the compound, pondering over what each new day would bring, their spirits sinking lower and lower.

Almost daily new groups of Indians arrived at the prison and were thrust into the already crowded confines. Where green grass once grew in the stockade there was now bare dirt, trampled by the footsteps of the huge number of prisoners. No privacy, people were everywhere.

Conditions within the tall walls worsened. During the hot dry weather, barrels of water, unsafe and unsanitary, grew dangerous to use. Sickness swept through the confines of the stockade daily. Slit trenches at opposite corners of the stockade, half-hidden by tarpaulins on pole frames, served as toilets. The stockade reeked of excrement and the sour smell of quicklime. Flies passed from the trenches to the food being served. The white government furnished the prisoners with wheat flour and dried meat. Since the Cherokee had not yet learned to bake bread, the women mixed the flour with water and made pancakes, but soon the cakes hardened becoming unchewable for the elderly. Some Cherokee had brought dried meat and parched corn, but they all wanted and needed fresh meat and vegetables.

Two babies had been born since White Feather arrived at the stockade and both infants died almost as soon as they entered the world. High fevers, measles and chicken pox swept through the stockade resulting in many of the children becoming seriously ill, some near death.

White Feather and Running Deer were grateful that Gv-nv-gc Yo-na and Little Fawn had remained healthy. But the children did not understand what was happening to them and sometimes they became cross and impatient, begging White Feather to let them go outside the gate to play.

A few of the Cherokee tried to escape as the soldiers opened the gates when they came into the stockade to perform various duties. The Indians were caught and thrown roughly back through the gates, often struck to the ground by blows from the blunt end of a soldier's rifle.

"The spirit has left our elders," White Feather thought. "Most are silent, staring into space, without noticing anything around them. They have resigned themselves."

"Please, Moon Face, please eat. You must be hungry," pleaded White Feather one morning, squatting down beside the old woman sitting on the ground. The younger woman placed a gentle hand on the elder's shoulder. "Please."

"No," Moon Face answered in a whisper.

"You must eat. You will get sick if you do not."

"I am not hungry."

"I will leave the food here," White Feather said, placing the food beside Moon Face. "Please, try to eat."

The old woman said nothing. She sat staring

toward the sky, waiting for the morning fog to lift so that she might see the mountains.

White Feather shook her head sadly, leaving Moon Face still gazing over the tall walls. She returned to Running Deer where he and the children were sitting on the bare ground trying to eat.

That night, a heavy rain fell on the stockade. During the early morning hours, something woke White Feather and she arose from the muddy ground. She heard the sound of laughter echoing through the quiet prison

"What is that?" thought White Feather, rubbing sleep from her eyes. "That's strange." She followed the sounds and saw a group of laughing children huddled around a young boy.

"...and we can play a trick on the soldier guarding the gate," the leader was saying to the other children.

"What kind of trick?" said one child.

The boy leaned close and spoke in a low voice. White Feather could not hear his words, but when he paused the children burst into laughter again.

She moved closer.

"Sh...you will have to be quiet," the leader instructed.

The children giggled.

"We will go to the gates. Each of you find a place where you can see between the poles. Be quiet and watch. Come!"

The children followed their leader to the gate while the curious White Feather trailed behind them. They pressed their faces close to the narrow openings between the poles, located the soldiers and waited.

Picking up a handful of mud, the leader patted it into a ball.

"Here goes," he whispered. "Watch!"

He leaned back and flung the mud ball over the gate toward the guard. It landed beside the military man, exploding into a burst of muddy water, spraying the guard's uniform.

"What the...?" the startled soldier exclaimed. He

wiped mud from his uniform, turned and saw eyes peering through the small openings in the stockade wall.

"Get away from here!" he yelled at the children. "That better not happen again!"

The children giggled while they watched the boy scoop up another handful of mud, cupping it in his hands to form a larger ball than the first.

"Here goes," he whispered, and tossed it over the gate.

Again mud sprayed the soldier's clothes as it landed near his feet.

The observers clapped their hands over their mouths to silence their laughter.

"All right!" the guard yelled, turning toward the children. "Don't do that again!"

"Watch THIS one," the boy said, forming another mud ball. He hurled it through the air.

This time the mud ball hit its target, splattering the face of the guard.

Bursting into loud laughter, the children ran away, leaving the military man wiping mud from his face and yelling angry threats.

White Feather watched the children go. "Sad...what our children will do here to feel alive. But...it is good to hear them laugh."

Then, suddenly, she laughed also.

CHAPTER TWENTY-ONE

Footprints in the Mud

White Feather sat on the damp, hard ground and looked at the people around her. Shifting her cold feet, she drew up her knees and folded her arms across them.

The days of confinement dragged slowly by and the nine or ten weeks since they had been herded into the compound seemed like an eternity.

"Our elders move about as if they are lost..." White Feather thought sadly, "...and bewildered. And Moon Face! Oh, poor Moon Face."

The older woman had stopped eating. No amount of coaxing and pleading from White Feather and Running Deer had been successful. Moon Face refused to take even a small amount. She had become extremely tired and weak and had spoken few words since arriving at the prison.

"Moon Face," White Feather had said, "Soon you'll see Tsu-la."

But she had not responded, simply staring over the wall. Her spirit broken, her will to live gone.

Two nights later she had silently laid down on

the ground and closed her eyes, never to open them again.

The next morning the soldiers had taken the body of Moon Face and that of a tiny infant who died at birth, outside the gates. White Feather prayed that Moon Face had received a proper burial. She would never know because none of the prisoners themselves were allowed outside the gates, even to bury their dead.

Suddenly, a soldier entered the stockade, calling out loudly, "Git yer thangs together. Yer leaving!"

White Feather's breath caught in her throat. "We're going home?" she thought.

"Yer leaving fer the Western Indian Territory! Now, git a move on! Daylight's a'wasting!"

Hope faded as White Feather's shoulders slumped.

"Come, White Feather," Running Deer said softly above her. "We must prepare to leave."

"No – no – no! I do not want to go," she said in panic. She did not move.

"Come," Running Deer urged again, taking his wife's hand to pull her to her feet.

Within the next half-hour, she and Running Deer gathered their few belongings and quickly fed Gv-nv-ge Yo-na and Little Fawn their last morsels of food. White Feather's face was grim.

The sound of Little Fawn crying drew White Feather out of her reverie.

Little Fawn stood before her, her cheeks wet with tears.

"I want to go home," Little Fawn whimpered. "I want to go home."

White Feather stooped and pulled the trembling child into her arms.

"I do too," she murmured to her daughter, hugging the child close.

"I want to go home," Little Fawn cried louder.

"Sh... sh," soothed White Feather, stroking the child's hair. "We will go back someday."

The huge gates swung open and soldiers poured into the stockade with rifles drawn.

"Move...Indians...Git going!" came the commands.

Over the top of the stockade wall White Feather could see the peaks of the mountains.

"We will be back," she promised softly. She set Little Fawn on the ground, picked up a bundle of their belongings and took her daughter's hand.

Lining up beside her husband who was carrying Gv-nv-ge Yo-na, the unhappy woman followed the other Cherokee as they made their way slowly out of the stockade.

There would be no turning back now...only soldiers and rifles and more soldiers.

Black clouds rolled in the sky. A hot wind moved through the forest surrounding the stockade, pushing against the empty barrier. In the quiet that comes just before a storm, jagged lightning lit up the ground and the footprints left behind in the mud.

CHAPTER TWENTY-TWO

The Ferry

When White Feather and the other Cherokee left the stockade they walked for two days before arriving at a huge camp at the edge of the river. There they joined hundreds of other Indians, all waiting to begin the long trek across the country.

White Feather, Running Deer and the children stood at the rail of the crowded ferry. They watched the dark water churn as the boat slowly pushed its way across the river to the Golconda Road where the journey to the west would continue.

"I am glad we left the camp by the river," said White Feather somberly, turning to look back toward the land they had just left.

"Yes," Running Deer responded. "It was bad there."

A child screamed nearby and began to cry.

White Feather looked at the child clinging to his mother's skirt. "He is afraid," she whispered to Running Deer.

"Many people on the boat are afraid. They fear

that the boat will sink from the heavy load it is carrying."

"Look at our children, Running Deer. They are not afraid," said White Feather nodding toward Gv-nv-ge Yo-na and Little Fawn. "They are brave. They are laughing and enjoying the ride."

"I will never forget the stench of the camp," White Feather continued, taking a deep breath of the fresh air. She turned her face toward the sky, took another deep breath and sighed.

Running Deer nodded in agreement.

"When we were leaving camp this morning, I thought I saw the captain who came to our village before the roundup," said White Feather thoughtfully. "Did you see him?"

"No."

"I suppose I could be mistaken. There were so many military men at the camp."

Suddenly, White Feather noticed a soldier standing by the rail, a stranger to her, staring at her. He smiled sadly, clearing his throat.

"We got eight hundred miles to go," he said.

CHAPTER TWENTY-THREE

Trapped Between Two Rivers

White Feather wrapped Gv-nv-ge Yo-na tightly in a blanket and laid him on the ground near the fire. She sat down, shivering, and tried to warm her cold body.

The long column of Cherokee had left the Tennessee River and marched through Tennessee and across Kentucky. Now they were camped by the Mississippi River, trapped between two rivers for ten days because the river was too dangerous to cross. There had been snow storms and the weather was bitter cold.

Travel had been difficult.

In late November the rain and mud had come again, followed by snow and harsh cold weather. There had been no shelter along the way and they had walked in the ice and snow. Many of her people, with their feet almost bare, had left bloody footprints on the icy ground.

White Feather thought about the suffering her people had been forced to endure. There had been sickness and deaths since the beginning of the terrible journey. The aged Cherokee and the children had pushed their bodies to the limit, suffering from physical exhaustion, many times dropping in the road, then pulling themselves up in fear of being left behind or separated from their family.

The wagons provided by the military for the aged and sick were filled to capacity.

The dreams of the Cherokee were gone, covered by mile after mile of footsteps. But, ironically, White Feather's fierce desire to live had grown stronger. She was alive, her family still together, and her determination steeled by the knowledge that she would somehow return home one day.

Running Deer had been sitting across the fire from White Feather holding Little Fawn in his arms. He stood and moved to White Feather's side.

"Are you getting warmer?" he asked.

She nodded, but did not speak; afraid her voice would betray the bitter coldness she really felt.

Running Deer sat beside White Feather and looked down at the girl he held. "She's suffering," he said.

Little Fawn had been ill for two days, her brow raging with fever. Her dark eyes were closed in sleep most of the time, springing open only when spasms of coughing hit.

"My heart aches for her," White Feather said, looking at the child.

"Yes. Were it not for this journey she would be laughing, running and playing," responded Running Deer softly, running a finger gently over Little Fawn's cheek.

"Today she seems to be worse than yesterday," White Feather said worriedly.

Running Deer nodded, pulling the child still closer to him. He remembered the joyful day of her birth back home. He recalled the morning well, and the sharing of his happiness with his friend, Tsu-la.

"Do you think we will ever see Tsu-la again, White Feather?"

She looked up, surprised that Running Deer

had mentioned their friend. "Tsu-la? Yes, perhaps."

"I wonder where he is today," said Running Deer. "Maybe he is happy now. I hope so." He missed his friend. The Indian man gazed into the burning embers, as images of the past clouded his mind.

White Feather lay sleeping in the cabin with her newborn daughter in her arms. Running Deer and Tsu-la sat on the porch, enjoying the sunrise together and rejoicing in the birth of the child.

Tsu-la pointed to the nearby woods and said, "Look, Running Deer, a little fawn has come out of the woods to greet your new daughter."

Running Deer smiled.

"A little fawn, a new young creature in this world also, just like my little one," Running Deer remained silent for a moment, then spoke. "I will name my child Little Fawn."

"A good name for a good child, my friend," Tsu-la said, looking at Running Deer and smiling. "It's the dawn of a new day. Look, the sun has risen to greet Little Fawn."

The men looked briefly at the sun peeking over the mountains and then watched the timid fawn return to the forest.

The fire flickered, then popped, interrupting Running Deer's thoughts.

"Little Fawn," he whispered softly. "I cannot bear the thought of you disappearing from my sight as the fawn disappeared so quickly on the morning of your birth." He leaned over and kissed the child's fevered brow.

Running Deer held her in his arms all night, lifting her head when the coughing spells came.

The following day the group was able to continue their journey. Running Deer carried Little Fawn in his arms as they continued westward, her fever and cough now interrupted with frequent chills.

When the march stopped for the night and a fire was built, Running Deer placed Little Fawn close to the small fire.

"I'm scared," White Feather spoke at his elbow. "So many children have died."

"She is so cold," Running Deer said. "She must have warmth." He quickly added his own blanket to cover the child.

"No!" protested White Feather loudly, looking at her husband's thinly clad body. "No. You cannot do this. Your blanket is your only covering against this terrible cold."

"She needs more warmth."

"No, Running Deer. It is snowing again," she said in alarm. "You must have a cover for your body."

"Little Fawn," he said softly, "fight hard." He sat by the fire, pulling the child closer to him and looked into White Feather's face. "She must get well," he whispered.

CHAPTER TWENTY-FOUR

The Grief of Loss

The following day Little Fawn began to improve. The coughing became less frequent and her fever subsided. But while Little Fawn became better, the weather became worse, colder; finally freezing the rivers.

As they resumed the walk, snow mixed with ice fell steadily and despite White Feather's insistence, Running Deer still refused to take his blanket from around Little Fawn.

The cold night air whipped across his near-naked body and on the third day without his blanket Running Deer became gravely ill. He tried to dismiss the ache in his body and the high fever but when the chills began White Feather ignored his resistance, and wrapped her own blanket around his shoulders.

But he did not improve; instead he became weaker.

Deep snow covered the ground and walking became more difficult and extremely dangerous. Deep ruts from the passing of the multitude of people, wagons and animals had been cut in the roads. Many of the Cherokee fell when they stepped in unseen holes covered with snow.

Each day Running Deer grew worse. White Feather tried to get him into a wagon, but sickness had continued to increase and there was no room in the wagons for any more people. Almost every day the procession of Cherokee paused to bury the dead along the road, and then move on.

When the march resumed early one icy morning White Feather noticed that Running Deer was having extreme difficulty walking. She stopped and took his hand.

"Let me pull your blanket across your chest," she said. "It has fallen down."

Her hand stopped in mid-air as it neared the blanket; she gasped in horror.

"Running Deer!" she whispered.

Terrified, she saw the entire front of his shirt stained with blood. She moved to pull the blanket around his neck. There were more bloodstains on the cover.

"We must stop and let you rest."

He shook his head and began moving again, his steps slower and more labored. White Feather pulled him to her and walked with her arm around him, supporting him as he walked.

"He should be in a wagon and have medicine," she thought angrily. "I hate this removal. I hate it!"

A strong gust of cold wind struck Running Deer and he paused, then tried to walk again. A few steps later, he fell.

White Feather screamed. She dropped to her knees beside him and placed her hand on his brow; the heat of his face burned her fingers.

With the support of White Feather's arm, slowly Running Deer pulled himself to his feet. He stumbled, and then fell in the tracks he had made in the snow. Blood oozed from his mouth.

"Running Deer...Running Deer...please don't leave!" On her knees again, the frightened woman wiped the blood away from his chin with her hand.

He said nothing, but laid still, his eyes closed.

"Live, Running Deer! Live!" White Feather begged.

The dying man slowly opened his eyes and tried to focus on White Feather's grief-stricken face. "C-c-come closer," he whispered.

"Sh...sh," White Feather's hands cupped his face. "Don't talk now." Desperately, she looked up from her husband, quickly noticing the frightened children huddling close. Dazed Cherokee shuffled past. She looked again at the man she loved.

He managed a slight smile while he fumbled at his thin shirt. He drew out a small leather pouch he had concealed. "Open it, White Feather," he whispered.

She looked questioningly into his face, "That's just your medicine pouch...what... what?" While she spoke, she had complied with his wishes. Inside the open pouch a rock gleamed gold within its dimness.

"Where did...?"

"Back home," interrupted Running Deer. "Remember...the day I left you for... most of the day...never told you where I went...."

"Yes," his wife whispered through tears as she gently stroked his fevered brow.

" ...went to our secret place...where we found the gold long ago...our secret... remember?"

"Yes," her voice quivered.

"This is for you. Use it; go back home...when the march is over." His voice broke as a spasm of coughing racked his body. More blood seeped from his mouth.

"No! Let me call a medicine man...there must be one here somewhere."

"No! Take the children home again...promise me...."

"I promise," White Feather said, softly crying.

"White Feather..." his voice so weak that she had to lean close to his mouth to hear his words. "I...love...you," he whispered, then closed his eyes.

"Running Deer?"

He did not answer.

"RUNNING DEER!"

Still no answer.

"NO! NO! NO!" White Feather screamed and fell across his lifeless body.

Seconds later, the stricken woman raised herself regally, gathered her dead husband fully into her arms and rocked him.

In the swirling snow, the land all around echoed as she raised her voice in sorrow.

Just to the side, Little Fawn drew her obedient brother underneath her blanket, holding him close. The two stood silent, huddled together, eyes wide in the grief of loss.

CHAPTER TWENTY-FIVE

Running Deer's Last Gift

Soldiers riding within earshot of White Feather heard the sound of her scream. The captain in charge slowed his horse and turned to the military man riding beside him.

"What's all the commotion back there, Sergeant?"

The sergeant turned in his saddle to look behind them and then swung back to face him. "Aw, Captain, it's probably one of the Injun women back there having another one of them babies we've got to drag along with us, Sir," the sergeant retorted indifferently.

"Well, go back there and see if you can help her," the captain responded, then added, "No, wait, I'll go myself."

White Feather's deep anguish had now drawn a group of Cherokee that had gathered around the family. Captain Howard pulled up on the reins, bringing his horse to a halt. "Do you need help?" he said.

White Feather looked up into the face of Captain Howard.

He was stunned at the sight of her. The grief-stricken woman was White Feather and he knew then that the still form lying on the ground must be Running Deer. He could not believe his eyes. He never expected to see them again.

White Feather did not respond, instead she turned back and pulled Running Deer tighter into her arms and continued to rock back and forth.

Two of the Indian women came forward, one lifted Little Fawn into her arms and the other reached for Gv-nv-ge Yo-na.

A young Cherokee man stepped forward and spoke to the captain. "We will carry Running Deer," he said, motioning to others.

"All right," answered the captain, "You can bury him tonight."

Deep in sadness, and not knowing what else to do, he nudged his horse and rode away to allow the people their privacy.

The quiet procession of Indians moved slowly past, their heads bowed in sorrow. Another one of their people would be buried in a nameless grave along this path to a strange unknown land.

White Feather, her body shaking from shock and cold, watched in silence while Running Deer was wrapped in his bloodstained blanket and lifted to be carried along with his people. Shock entered her body with such a force that she refused to believe Running Deer was really gone. "It simply is not so! Only a short time ago he was walking beside me! Oh, Running Deer," she sobbed bringing her hand to her chest.

She suddenly realized that she held a stone in her hand. "The nugget...the gold. I had forgotten about it." She fingered the hard stone, remembering Running Deer's words. "He's given us our way home," she thought. "His last gift."

In the power of the moment, a gentle hand touched her shoulder.

"Come, White Feather. It is time to go."

"Yes. I must go with Running Deer," she said. Placing the string of the rawhide pouch around her neck, she fell into step with the woman.

"White Feather, I am Singing Bird and this is Sa-lo-li (Gray Squirrel), my husband," the older woman said, pointing to the man who walked beside them. "We will help you. We have had death in our family on the trail too. We understand how you feel. Our daughter died with a strange sickness soon after we began the walk. Now we will take you as our daughter, if you will let us. We are of the same Cherokee Paint Clan."

White Feather touched the woman on her arm, trying to smile. Then, within the sound of many footsteps in the snow, the widowed woman gazed at the bundle being carried before her. "Running Deer," she vowed in her mind. "I will finish this trip. But, I promise you! I will take our children back to the land of our ancestors."

Then she stepped forward again, toward the land of the setting sun.

CHAPTER TWENTY-SIX

Bitter Cold Determination

Snow fell. The bitter-cold wind blew. Thinly-clad Cherokee inched their way onward. Days had passed since Running Deer's burial, and White Feather had continued the march in silence. She spoke only when absolutely necessary. She took care of her children, when they were not with Singing Bird and Sa-lo-li, attending to their needs.

Little Fawn, the happy, laughing child of the mountains was now silent, withdrawn, crying often. She missed her father carrying her, holding her hand while they walked along the road. Each time she asked for Running Deer, White Feather could only reply, "He's gone."

White Feather's head bent low. Her eyes saw nothing but the icy-white snow beneath her cold feet. She pulled Gv-nv-ge Yo-na closer in her arms while the child slept, then glanced behind her, quickly looking for Little Fawn. Satisfied when she saw her being carried by Sa-lo-li, she nodded to the old man. She was grateful for the help from the couple and had grown to love them as family.

Over and over, the grieving woman touched the pouch around her neck. How did Running Deer expect her to use it to return home, she wondered. No Indian was supposed to have gold; at least that is what the white people thought when they made it against the law for an Indian to pan for gold back in the mountains. No one must ever know her secret about the nugget. What lay ahead for White Feather in the new land was unknown, but her promise to Running Deer was embedded in her heart and would not be broken.

"Running Deer, I miss you beside me," she whispered. Her footsteps paused and a gust of cold wind suddenly struck her face. "I must be strong. I must think of happier times...keep my thoughts from becoming too sad," White Feather thought. "I must go on. Little Fawn and Gv-nv-ge Yo-na have lost one parent, they must not lose another," she promised herself and tried to pull her shoulders erect to stand tall against the weather elements threatening to halt her in her tracks.

Happier times...long ago."We were happy then," she thought, feeling a lump form in her throat. In her musings, White Feather slipped back in time to her wedding day.

Joy covered Running Deer's face as they moved toward each other and met in the center of the council house near the sacred fire. They wore blue blankets around their shoulders representing their old lives and old ways. He smiled deep into her heart.

As they exchanged gifts with each other, the white blanket was placed around their shoulders, symbolizing their union and uniting them into one household. They sipped the corn drink from the double-sided wedding vase and then threw the vase down, breaking it to seal their wedding vows, returning the fragments to Mother Earth to be recreated into a new life. They laughed and slipped away, while the wedding feast had gone on and on....late into the night.

Gv-nv-ge Yo-na cried out in her arms. She

pulled his body closer, hoping to warm the cold child. "The children are tired and hungry." She hugged Gv-nv-ge Yo-na close again, whispering, "Be strong, my son. We will survive this terrible time and go home again."

With her head bent, she saw the footprints of the Cherokee in the snow, those of her people who walked before her, some of them leaving blood from feet that wore no moccasins.

White Feather placed her own feet into those impressions, into the footprints of blood.

CHAPTER TWENTY-SEVEN

Survivors

Flickering campfires dotted the dark countryside where the Cherokee camped for the night. Captain Howard sat alone beside one of the fires, staring into the burning embers. So far, this had been the most difficult six months of his life; a memory that would burn in his heart for the rest of his days.

He shivered, pulling the collar of his coat close-ly around his neck to keep out the cold wind. The journey had been harsh and cruel. He shook his head sadly, remembering the countless graves along the roadside across the country. Cherokee were buried nearly everyday, their lives claimed by the march.

The journey had been made at the most difficult time of the year. There had been extreme drought, then heavy rains leaving water on the ground followed by snow and freezing weather.

Somewhere close by a small child's crying pierced the quiet countryside and Captain Howard's eyes searched through the darkness toward the pitiful wails.

"The child is probably hungry...or sick," he

thought. Sickness had accompanied the group during the entire journey.

Captain Howard rose and stirred the fire. Heavily he sank back down on the cold ground, sighing deeply. "So much has happened," he murmured.

Out of his group more than one hundred refugees had fled into the woods during the first few nightly camps. Mothers had given birth along the roadsides as hundreds of Cherokee and soldiers passed by, glancing at the event with curiosity, then turning away in embarrassment. Food had been scarce. The government had issued corn and salt pork almost everyday, but it had not been sufficient to prevent the deaths resulting from starvation and sickness, especially among the Cherokee elders and children. And still sickness remained among the survivors.

The captain pulled his coat collar higher as another blast of cold wind whipped across him and threatened to extinguish his small campfire. He glanced out toward the glowing fires and at the people huddled around them.

"They are weak in body and sick at heart," he thought. "And they have received emotional scars."

Exhaustion had overtaken the survivors and the procession had moved slower and slower during the past few weeks. The Captain would never forget the desperate faces of the people as they pushed their bodies to the limits of endurance to reach their destination.

The logs shifted, sparking. The fire had burned down. The Captain stood and placed another log on the dying embers.

CHAPTER TWENTY-EIGHT

Arrival in the Western Indian Territory

White Feather sighed, "Finally...finally...we can stop. I am so tired of walking." Wearily she sank to the ground, took the children's hands and pulled them down beside her.

Gv-nv-ge Yo-na and Little Fawn sat and leaned heavily against their mother. Exhausted and silent, they fell asleep almost instantly.

White Feather rubbed her aching legs and swollen feet, trying to survey her new surroundings. The land was pretty, she admitted to herself, but there were no mountains.

She closed her eyes. She had almost fallen asleep when a gentle hand touched her shoulder.

"Come, White Feather," a soft voice beckoned above her. "Come with us."

"Where?" she asked sleepily, not looking up.

"Come. You will come with us."

Caring hands picked up the sleeping children.

"Sa-lo-li and Singing Bird, my friends," she said, "you've helped me on the long journey, especially with the children. Thank you."

Smiling, the two motioned for her to come.

The trip had been difficult for the old couple. She wanted to weep for them. White Feather pushed herself up and glanced around.

Now that they had arrived at their destination most of the Indians were confused, not sure what they were to do next. They stood silently as if waiting for more orders. Some sat on the ground resting, needing to sleep.

"Let us go on," Sa-lo-li urged.

"Where will we go?" White Feather questioned as they walked away from the crowd toward a road. "Wait!" she added, "Let me carry Gv-nv-ge Yo-na." She took the sleeping child and gazed into Singing Bird's tired face. "You rest," she said and followed behind them. "Where will we go?" she asked again.

"We will find a place," said Sa-lo-li. "Some of the old settlers may help us."

"The old settlers?" asked White Feather. "Who are they?"

"They are our Cherokee people who chose to come to the new territory many years ago," answered Sa-lo-li. "Even before the time Tsu-la, your friend, came here."

"Chose to come here?" thought White Feather. "Why would they choose to leave our homeland in the east?" She shook her head in disbelief as they walked down the road.

Suddenly Singing Bird stumbled, almost falling. She grabbed her chest, her breath rapid and labored. Perspiration covered her brow.

"Singing Bird! What is it?" White Feather cried in alarm, running to the old woman's side. "What is wrong?"

"It will pass, " Singing Bird gasped, moving her hand from her chest to rub the inside of her arm.

"You must rest," White Feather pleaded.

"We will stop," said Sa-lo-li.

"No. It has happened before," murmured Singing Bird. "The pain will go away." She paused for a moment, then continued down the road.

White Feather frowned. Concern and worry for her friends pulled at her heart. "I must be their strength now," she thought.

She moved quickly around the old couple and turned to face them, stopping them in the road.

"Singing Bird, Sa-lo-li...it is my turn to help you. Now you must let me help you."

She smiled; the first time she had smiled in a long, long time.

"You are as our daughter," Singing Bird said brokenly.

"Now, come," White Feather said brightly. "Come. I will lead the way," she set off, not knowing where the road would take them.

CHAPTER TWENTY-NINE

Getting Settled

White Feather leaned back and squinted toward the cloudless sky. "The sun feels good," she said. "I'm glad we have a warm day."

"Yes," Singing Bird answered. "There were times on the trail when I thought I would never be warm again."

White Feather nodded in agreement.

The two women lounged lazily on the steps of the small cabin porch, enjoying the sunlight while they watched Little Fawn and Gv-nv-ge Yo-na playing in the yard.

They sat in silence for a moment, each lost in her own thoughts about their new home in the western territory.

It had been a month since they had arrived. By mere chance, they had met a kind young Indian couple who were eager to help them. The couple, whose parents had been among the first families to settle the western territory, had given them enough food to last for several days and had taken them to a small abandoned house. The cabin, half-hidden in the undergrowth, had been not much more than a shack. It had no furnishings, but it was a welcome haven for the exhausted refugees who were grateful to have a roof over their heads. The couple left them and returned later in the day with two blankets, a small table, some chairs and a few clothes for the children. Their support and that of other settled Cherokee helped to build their strength again.

"It is good that Sa-lo-li found work," said Singing Bird, "and so soon."

White Feather nodded.

"Someday we might have enough money to buy beds," Singing Bird chuckled.

"And have our own corn husks to sleep on!" White Feather said.

"Yes, but we have been fortunate," said White Feather. "Much more so than some of our Cherokee brothers sleeping under the stars."

"Perhaps some of the baskets you have woven will sell someday," said Singing Bird hopefully. "They are beautiful."

White Feather's gaze took in the baskets sitting on the porch. They were not of the honeysuckle and white oak she had used in the mountains.

"It took much searching to find the buck bush, but I am pleased," she said.

"Maybe Sa-lo-li can sell them for you," Singing Bird said, "now that he is working at the store in town."

White Feather thought a moment, then responded, "His wages are small...this could help buy food until we can plant."

"Sa-lo-li has told me that the white store owner and his Indian son-in-law have treated him kindly."

"A Cherokee works with Sa-lo-li?"

"Sa-lo-li said he arrived before the forced removal began, but that's all he knows.

"I would like to meet him," White Feather said. "Maybe he knows Tsu-la!"

With renewed energy the young Indian woman reached for an unfinished basket and began weaving.

Later in the day White Feather still sat lost in her work, while Singing Bird bent over the pot of stew simmering on the outside fire. Suddenly, White Feather saw the old woman gasp for breath.

Running to Singing Bird, terror griped White Feather as her friend held her chest, struggling to breathe.

"Go, White Feather...go get Sa-lo-li...need him here with me," Singing Bird whispered weakly as she sank to the ground.

"Little Fawn!" cried White Feather. "Take care of Gv-nv-ge Yo-na! Stay here with Singing Bird! I will be back soon. Do not leave her! Stay by her side!"

The bewildered children came quickly to Singing Bird.

"I will return soon," White Feather said to Singing Bird and ran down the road.

Glancing back over her shoulder, the last image she saw was Singing Bird stretched out on the ground with the children standing over her.

Bursting through the door of the store, White Feather cried out. "Sa-lo-li! Sa-lo-li, where are you?" Urgency pushed her further into the dim interior. Again, she cried out, "Sa-lo-li!"

A wide-eyed Sa-lo-li came running from the back room.

"It is Singing Bird! She needs you! She clutched her chest and fell to the ground. You must go!"

Without a sound, Sa-lo-li was gone.

White Feather whirled and left the store, following in his wake.

CHAPTER THIRTY

A Sour and A Sweet Time

A lone figure stood in the shadow of the door of the mercantile store, and watched the retreating White Feather.

"They're here," Tsu-la thought, and his heart grew full. After a moment, he called over his shoulder. "My father-in-law, I must go to help!"

"Wait, Tsu-la," said Mr. Wade. "I'll close the store and go with you. Sa-lo-li may need us."

Sa-lo-li arrived too late to bid Singing Bird good-bye. Dropping to the ground, he lifted her head into his lap and rocked back and forth. Little Fawn and Gv-nv-ge Yo-na sat quietly on the grass, slowly realizing the death of yet another loved one.

White Feather rushed up, understanding without words the loss of her friend. She sank beside Sa-lo-li.

It was into this scene of sorrow that the two men came. Breathing heavy, they stood back in respect, sharing the loss.

After what seemed like hours, Sa-lo-li acknowledged the presence of the men, and then stood, lifting
his wife into his arms and carried her into the cabin.

"White Feather," said Tsu-la to the bowed head
of his friend, "White Feather...it is Tsu-la!"

With a gasp, the suddenly stunned woman
looked up.

"Tsu-la!" she cried. "It is you!"

Sa-lo-li came out of the house to stand on the
porch, as White Feather rose and ran into the arms of
her husband's best friend, and then burst into tears.

After a moment, Tsu-la addressed his companion over her head.

"Mr. Wade, this is White Feather from my homeland. She and her husband, Running Deer, are my
dearest friends from the mountains."

"I'm glad to meet you, White Feather," he said
extending his hand as the woman stood back and
wiped her eyes. "Tsu-la has spoken of you many
times."

Caught between the sadness and happiness of
the moment, White Feather nodded to Mr. Wade, con-
tinuing to stare at Tsu-la.

"Can I help you, Sa-lo-li? Is there anything I
can do?" Mr. Wade's attention had turned to the
grieving man on the porch.

"I will need time to be with my wife."

"Take all the time you want. Please let me know
of your arrangements. I would like to come." And
then, to Tsu-la, Mr. Wade continued, "I will leave you
to help the family, Tsu-la...I'll go on back to the store."

"Ski (thank you)," Tsu-la said, and as Mr. Wade
nodded again to White Feather, he walked back down
the road.

Tsu-la then turned back to White Feather.
"Where is Running Deer?"

Tears filled White Feather's eyes. "Running Deer
is dead."

"Dead?" Tsu-la stepped back and stared at her
in disbelief. "Dead?"

"Yes...during the walk on the trail here he left

us. And now Singing Bird has joined him."

CHAPTER THIRTY-ONE

The Changing Winds

A week passed, an extremely sad week for White Feather. She remembered how Singing Bird had pushed her body to survive the long trek across the country. In doing so, it had taken her strength, her health, and finally her life.

Sa-lo-li remained in the cabin for four days after his wife's death but now he, too, was gone.

The night after Singing Bird's burial Mr. Wade and Tsu-la had come to the cabin. The conversation that night had changed all their lives. Sa-lo-li would become the watchman at the store and live in the back room.

It was difficult for Sa-lo-li to leave. White Feather watched while he gathered his few clothes, laid them on his blanket and folded the blanket around them; then he placed the bundle under his arm. He looked at her and smiled, hugged the children and walked out of the cabin and down the steps.

White Feather ran out on the porch and called after him. "Wait, wait, Sa-lo-li!"

She ran to the old man and hugged him.

He turned and walked slowly away.

"We will see you soon, Sa-lo-li," she called to him. "Take care of yourself."

Glancing over his shoulder he waved and managed a smile.

The next few days had been lonely without the elders around but Tsu-la had come every day to visit when he closed the store. He loved playing with the children and delighting them with little gifts.

On one of his first visits he espied the beautiful baskets White Feather had woven and insisted on taking them to the store to sell. Almost daily he returned with money for White Feather from her basket sales.

One afternoon the two friends sat on the cabin's porch watching the children play and talking about their past lives in the mountains until dusk turned into night.

"White Feather, let me tell you about my life here in the west," Tsu-la said.

"Please," White Feather replied, "tell me all that has happened."

"When I arrived here, I was surprised at how quickly I came to know my surroundings. I found a job in Mr. Wade's mercantile store. He was very kind to me and let me live in the back room of the store where Sa-lo-li lives now; it was good there. I cleaned and ran errands too, like Sa-lo-li does. I was glad to have a job. The pay was good," he chuckled. "Mr. Wade was very kind to me and we became close friends.

"Eventually I was given more responsibility in the store and worked long hours. I liked my work but I was lonely, especially when I went into my little room after the store closed each day.

"One day Mr. Wade's young daughter, his only child, and her little girl visited the store for supplies. Her husband had passed away." He smiled. "'That is how I met Marie. She lived with her father and she began coming to the store often and we became friends. Later she invited me to meet them at church on Sundays, which I did, and soon she and Mr. Wade began inviting me home with them for dinner after church."

Tsu-la continued telling White Feather how the friendship progressed quickly to love and they had married within a year.

"I moved into Mr. Wade's house because Marie and her father wanted me to, and since Mr. Wade was alone and in failing health, the arrangement has worked well." Tsu-la paused. "Mr. Wade has now given me the complete responsibility of managing the business...he still visits the store every afternoon. And I have a little girl now...Gloria."

"You are happy in your new life, aren't you, Tsu-la?"

"Yes. The sad times are memories. The move has been good for me, but I do miss our homeland. I plan to go back someday for a visit."

White Feather smiled at Tsu-la, rubbing the pouch around her neck.

"I have something else to be grateful for," said Tsu-la.

"What?"

"Marie and I are going to have a little one...it will be jumping down soon."

"A baby?"

"Yes!"

"That's wonderful, Tsu-la," she laughed, hugging him.

"It is, but Marie has not been well. Doc Lee is caring for her...she is not strong."

"Does she have help, Tsu-la?"

"No. She needs you." He grinned, a twinkle in his eyes.

"Me?"

"Yes, you! Marie and I, and Mr. Wade, want you and the children to come live with us."

"Oh, I could not do that, Tsu-la."

"We have plenty of room. We...Marie needs you. We have no one else."

"But, I...."

Tsu-la interrupted White Feather. "White Feather," he said, taking her hand in both of his, "you will love Marie and Gloria and I know that they will love you and your children."

"But...."

"She's a fine woman with much love to give."

"I know, but..."

"She knows of our friendship back in the east and," he paused, "she knows of the cruelty our people have suffered."

"She...."

"We've discussed your coming to live with us."

"Mr. Wade too?"

"Yes. Marie is anxious to meet you. Please say you will come."

"Well, I...."

"And," Tsu-la interrupted, "Little Fawn and Gv-nv-ge Yo-na will have someone to play with them."

Finally White Feather consented. "Having a home and food...and being near Tsu-la...that will be good," she thought.

"I will bring the buckboard for you and the children early in the morning," Tsu-la said cheerfully as he left.

White Feather sat on the porch waiting for Tsu-la's arrival. Her few possessions were neatly stacked nearby.

The children had been awake for hours and now sat on the steps anxiously watching the road for Tsu-la's arrival. They were excited about going to live at Tsu-la's house and meeting Gloria.

The sound of hooves and wagon wheels alerted White Feather to Tsu-la 's arrival, approaching in a cloud of dust, waving his hand to them and smiling broadly. He pulled on the reins and stopped the wagon in front of the cabin.

"Good morning, everyone," he said brightly, jumping from the wagon.

The children squealed, then ran to him, shouting his name.

He lifted Little Fawn into his arms.

"You have grown since yesterday, little one," he smiled at her then put her down beside her brother.

"Come," he said to Gv-nv-ge Yo-na.

Gv-nv-ge Yo-na smiled as he was lifted into the air.

Tsu-la's heart warmed when he looked into the child's face and recognized how much Gv-nv-ge Yo-na resembled his father.

He reached down and took Little Fawn's hand. "Come. We are going home," he said lightly. "There are people waiting anxiously to meet you."

CHAPTER THIRTY-TWO

Friendship

Marie smiled. "It sounds beautiful," she said. "It is, Marie," White Feather responded, her eyes sparkling, remembering the beauty of her homeland.

"I want to go there someday," Marie replied, "to see the mountains. Please, White Feather, tell me more about your life in the east."

The two women had become friends immediately during their first meeting and spent many afternoons on the porch exchanging information about their lives, all the while watching the children in the yard.

White Feather had told her new friend about Running Deer, their cabin in the mountains beside the river, the friendship with Tsu-la and the happy times they had spent together with her Cherokee people.

Marie enjoyed everything White Feather told her about the Cherokee way of life, but she noticed that White Feather never spoke of the walk across the country leading from her home. She was careful not to mention the exile during their conversations.

"Your life here, Marie...how was it before you

met Tsu-la?" White Feather said.

"Well, where do you want me to begin?" laughed Marie.

"Anywhere," answered White Feather.

"When my mother died I was very young, even younger than our children are now. My father raised me. When I grew up, I married a man I had known since childhood. We lived in town and were happy, but he died after we were married for three years."

"Oh," White Feather said, placing her hand on Marie's arm, remembering the death of her own husband. "I am so sorry."

"Thank you, " she said, then continued. "Gloria was only a few months old at the time and father insisted that we move here and live with him. I've been here ever since."

"Your father helped you," White Feather said kindly.

"Well, you know, White Feather," she said, pausing briefly and looking at the children. "I had never planned to marry again after my husband died, but when I met Tsu-la I changed my mind." she smiled.

"I am glad," White Feather smiled at her new friend.

"Tsu-la has made me happy...even happier now." Marie patted her stomach.

"Tsu-la was sad a long time."

"I am deeply in love with him. He is a good man, a good husband. My father thinks so, also...for he's now given the store over to him."

White Feather sat silent. Her mind wrapped itself around the thought of how could this be? A white man trusting an Indian!

Marie continued, "But, the responsibility causes Tsu-la to stay away more. I'm so glad you're here...and that you're my friend."

For a time, the two women sat quietly, lost in their thoughts, absently watching the children who had become playmates.

Marie, in her reverie, had suddenly realized that

her forthcoming child would be a Cherokee. She smiled at the thought that Gloria, her fair-skinned, blond, blue-eyed white girl would have a brown-skinned black-eyed brother or sister. Warm happiness swept over her.

Beside Marie, White Feather's gaze had slipped from the children to the horizon of the flat land of this new territory. A haze had risen in the distance, climbing into the image of home. Determination crawled into her eyes.

CHAPTER THIRTY-THREE

Michael

White Feather heard a light knock at the door and Tsu-la welcoming the visitor.

When the man's voice responded White Feather paused to listen and her hands froze in mid-air over the bowl of food she was preparing.

"No!" she whispered in disbelief. "It is my imagination. It can't be him!"

The stunned woman stood transfixed, listening to the conversation in the living room.

"So, how's your new house coming?" Tsu-la was saying. "It's keeping you so busy that we haven't seen you lately."

The man chuckled. "Just about as much as the livery business. It's hard juggling the running of a business and building a cabin."

"You need the cabin...can't raise a family in a livery stable."

"What family?" Marie said, coming into the room.

The men laughed.

"The one he doesn't know he's going to have," Tsu-la said.

"White Feather," called Marie, "Come and meet Michael."

The woman in the kitchen couldn't move, nor could she speak. She did not answer.

Suddenly, Marie stood in the doorway. "Michael is here," she said. "Come and meet our friend."

And then Tsu-la pushed around Marie, calling over his shoulder. "White Feather is making supper, Michael. Come on out here and meet someone very special to me."

As the tall man entered the room behind the Cherokee, Tsu-la continued. "Michael, this is White Feather." He paused, and then, indicating with his arm, he said, "White Feather, this is Michael Howard."

Slowly, White Feather looked into the eyes of Captain Howard.

CHAPTER THIRTY-FOUR

Retreating from Pain

White Feather and Michael stood motionless, facing each other, neither one believing their eyes. Seeing the look on White Feather's face, Marie placed a hand on her shoulder.

"Michael was on the march with the Cherokee from the east," she said gently, "Did you know him?"

Still White Feather did not move or respond but continued to stare at Michael in disbelief.

"Are you all right, Michael?" Tsu-la said, and then smiled. "I told you she was beautiful."

Regaining his composure, Michael finally spoke.

"White Feather," he said, "I'm happy to see you again." he managed a quick smile.

"Captain," she murmured softly, casting her eyes downward.

"Not Captain. Michael's not in the army anymore," Tsu-la said.

The awkward silence between White Feather and Michael continued as Marie and Tsu-la looked on in bewilderment.

"Do you know each other?" Marie said again.

"Yes," White Feather said and then quickly retreated to the stove. "Why don't you all sit at the table. I'll bring supper."

As the three left the room, White Feather leaned against the wall in the kitchen, trembling, and shuddering in disbelief. Captain Howard...here! She had never expected to see him again. Hearing the soft conversation in the dining room she was reminded that she would be expected to join them. She hurriedly walked back and forth from the kitchen to the dining room, filling the table with food. She could feel Captain Howard's eyes following her every move. Finally, she sat down, remaining silent during the meal, speaking only when absolutely necessary. Her mind whirled...this was Tsu-la's friend called Michael she had heard so much about. She knew him only as Captain Howard. Seeing him again had sent a shock of pain through her body. He represented the brutal walk from the east. The remembrance of it was almost unbearable to White Feather...even now. She pushed the food around on her plate and pretended to eat, occasionally glancing briefly at the man sitting across from her.

And then, slowly, it all came back...the physical pain, the loss of her husband, the illness all around her, the walk. This man represented everything she had endured. But, she had lived and her children had lived. This man was the soldier who had come to her and her children offering his help when Running Deer died. He had been kind to her on the trail. Seeing Captain Howard had opened all the painful memories in her mind of leaving her home, the agony for her people and her own hurt of losing Running Deer. She looked down at the plate of food in front of her. She tried to eat but the food would not pass the lump in her throat. She sat quietly fighting the tears begging to be released.

Marie and Tsu-la continued to make conversation, talking around the two.

"This is painful," Michael thought, stealing a

glance across the table at White Feather. " The look
on her face I have felt before. The pain that I have
carried in my heart for all these months...there it is on
her face. It's the tragedy of the human race, and I'm
part of it. How I hate it! This woman has come
through it all...she's bringing back the suffering I've
worked so hard to forget. There must be a reason for
all of this!"

"Michael?" Tsu-la's voice interrupted his thoughts.
"Uhhh...yes?" Michael responded, embarrassed,
"you were saying?"
     "I was asking, my friend, if the meal was satis-
factory to your taste?" Tsu-la laughed.
"Oh, yes, yes! Please excuse my bad manners," he
said, looking down to see his empty plate, not realizing
that he had finished eating his meal. "The supper was
delicious."
"White Feather prepared the meal for us. She's a
good cook." Marie smiled toward White Feather.
"I couldn't eat another bite," he said, and swal-
lowed his surfacing guilt.
"I'm glad you liked it," White Feather answered
softly, not looking up from her lap, wondering if the
meal would ever end.
Then, Tsu-la and Michael rose, and Tsu-la led the
way to the porch.
White Feather immediately busied herself cleaning
off the table. She hurried between the table and the
kitchen with Marie following her every step, curiously
questioning her behavior.
"White Feather, since you cooked supper, let me
clean up," Marie said, taking the dishes from her
hands. "What is wrong? You were so quiet during
supper. Are you ill?"
"No."
"Then what is it? Didn't you like Michael?"
"He seems like a nice man," replied White Feather,
not wishing to hurt her friend's feelings.
"He is. He's a very nice man; he's good, he's
kind," assured Marie. She paused, searching White

Feather's face for an answer. "Tsu-la and I had hoped you would like him."

When White Feather did not respond Marie put her hands on her shoulders and turned the Indian woman to face her.

"White Feather," she said seriously, "you did know Michael during the trip from your home, didn't you?"

White Feather sighed and dropped her head. "Yes, I told you before that I knew him," she answered.

"Did he hurt you?" Marie asked, remembering the horrible stories she had heard in town about the abuse some of the Indians had received from soldiers on the march.

"No, he was very kind," White Feather said, looking into Marie's eyes.

"Oh, I don't even know why I asked such an absurd question, knowing Michael as well as I do. He would never be unkind to anyone."

Marie paused, dropped her hands from White Feather's shoulders and hoped that her friend would explain her behavior.

White Feather turned and went to get a bucket of water on a nearby table to pour over the dishes, not speaking.

Marie persisted, "Then what is wrong? Can't you tell me?"

"I do not dislike Captain Howard but his presence reminds me of what his government did to my people...he reminds me of Running Deer's death," White Feather explained.

"I'm so sorry....but, Michael was not responsible, darling," Marie said compassionately. "It's over now. You must try to forget what has happened in the past." Marie quickly began washing the dishes. "You must now try to build a new life here for yourself and your children."

"Yes," White Feather said, and thought, "but not here in the west."

"Now, come," Marie said brightly, taking White Feather's hand, "we'll leave the dishes to dry. Let's go sit on the porch with the men and enjoy the evening."

"You go, Marie. I am tired."

"Well, come sit and rest."

"I do not mean to be rude, Marie, but please, go without me."

"Are you sure you won't join us?"

"Yes."

"Maybe later?" asked Marie, still hopeful of getting Michael and White Feather together.

White Feather dropped her head and moved it from side to side, refusing Marie's invitation. Her friend sighed and turned to walk out of the room.

"Marie...."

"Yes?" she said, turning to White Feather, hoping that she had changed her mind.

"Please tell your friend good night for me."

"Yes, of course."

White Feather was exhausted from the strain of seeing the captain again. It had been a very difficult evening for her but now she would put it behind her.

She tiptoed into her bedroom, careful not to wake her sleeping children who shared the room with her. She undressed and slipped into her bed, welcoming the comfort to her tired body. She stretched full length on her back and raised her hand to the hidden pouch with the gold nugget lying on her chest.

Glancing over at her children, she whispered, "We will go home soon, my little ones."

CHAPTER THIRTY-FIVE

Understanding White Feather

Marie and Tsu-la watched Michael ride away, stooped over in his saddle looking forlorn and sad. When he faded from their sight Tsu-la spoke. "I do not understand why White Feather didn't talk during supper."

Marie continued to rock gently in her chair, remaining quiet while Tsu-la spoke.

"I have known her since she was a child. This is not like her."

"She has known him before," Marie offered softly.

"What do you mean...known him?" Tsu-la questioned, turning to look at Marie.

"She knew him on the march here."

"Knew him?"

"Yes."

"Did he harm her?" Tsu-la asked, then raced on without waiting for an answer. "If he did, I'll...."

"No. No," Marie interrupted. "She admitted to me that he was very kind to her."

"Kind to her? Well, then why would she behave as she did in his presence?" Tsu-la paused. "Are you sure that he did not hurt her?"

"Yes. She told me that he was very good to her when Running Deer died."

"My people who made the walk have told me how Michael helped them. We both know how he feels about what the government did to the Indians in the east," said Tsu-la.

"Yes, but, nonetheless, Michael reminds White Feather of the removal and all the sadness."

"But she cannot blame every soldier who served in the army for the removal. Many of them hated the job that was assigned to them. I have heard them speak of it; many of the military men were very kind to my people."

"Yes, but seeing Michael reminds White Feather of the walk and all the unhappiness."

"Yes, but...."

"I think we should leave her to fight this battle alone," said Marie, "but we can be here to support her. She has suffered much in her young life. She misses Running Deer terribly."

"Yes, I'm sure she does. I miss him too," Tsu-la added. "We can try to help her build a new life for herself and her children. Running Deer would want that. Someday White Feather will want her own home again."

The couple became silent, each thinking about the young woman and her future.

"Do you think White Feather will ever smile again?" Marie asked. "I have never heard her laugh."

"She has a beautiful laugh. I wish you could have known her when Running Deer...." His voice faded off.

CHAPTER THIRTY-SIX

Grief Revisited

White Feather had stayed busy during the following days after she had seen Michael. She worked hard in the house trying to rid her mind of him, but she thought of Michael often, more often than she liked. Captain Howard...Michael. He was a gentleman, very polite. Kind.

"I should try to see him in a different light," she often scolded herself during the days after his visit. "He is Tsu-la and Marie's friend. I will probably not see him much.... Oh, I want the days to pass quickly. I want Marie's baby to arrive. Tomorrow...will be a better day."

The next afternoon while Marie was resting in her bed, White Feather took the three children into the living room to play, but after a short time Gloria got up and joined her mother to take a nap.

Soon Gv-nv-ge Yo-na climbed into his mother's lap and fell asleep. When White Feather left the room to put him in his bed Little Fawn wandered out onto the front porch.

Just as White Feather returned to the living room she heard Little Fawn's scream, followed by crying. Frightened, she ran toward the weeping child and when she reached the porch the crying had already diminished to low sobs. White Feather stopped abruptly. Captain Howard stood at the foot of the steps holding Little Fawn in his arms and soothing away the hurt from her fall down the steps.

Michael looked up, smiling at White Feather. "I was just riding into the yard when Little Fawn ran to meet me; however, she didn't quite make it to the bottom step. She's not hurt badly," he said, "just a little frightened." Turning to look at Little Fawn, he stroked the child's head and asked softly, "Do you feel better now, little one?"

Little Fawn nodded her head.

Michael smiled and reached into his coat pocket and withdrew a small bag and handed it to Little Fawn.

"Candy always seems to help a little," he smiled up at White Feather who stood motionless watching the scene.

Michael laughed when Little Fawn hugged him, all tears forgotten.

White Feather regained her composure and moved down the steps quickly and took her daughter from Michael. She cradled the child in her arms, relieved. She turned toward Michael. "Thank you, Captain," she said as she bounded up the steps. When she reached the porch she heard Michael's voice calling after her.

"Wait, White Feather, wait! I want to talk to you."

Afraid of facing her relenting feelings, White Feather did not acknowledge that she had heard him. She ran into the house quickly, never looking back.

"And I wish you would call me Michael," he called loudly as she quickly disappeared from his sight.

White Feather hesitated briefly then continued on toward her bedroom. On her way she passed Marie who had awakened at the commotion on the porch and gotten out of bed.

"White Feather, what happened?"

"It's nothing," White Feather casually threw over her shoulder and walked into her room closing the door behind her.

"What...?"

She met Michael in the front doorway. "Michael, what in the world happened?"

Quickly he explained the incident and then added, "Why won't she talk to me, Marie?"

Marie placed her hand comfortingly on Michael's shoulder. "Be patient, Michael. Give her time."

"The captain...back again," White Feather thought as she bathed Little Fawn's injured knees. "I will stay in here until he leaves."

Little Fawn pulled her mother's dress sleeve to gain her attention, interrupting White Feather's thoughts.

"I like Michael. He is nice. He brought me candy. See?" Little Fawn held out her small hand clutching the bag Michael had given her.

"I see," White Feather, muttered, "it was a nice thing for him to do."

After meeting Michael again White Feather refused to leave the house for anything, even to go to church on Sundays--her grief kept her home. The three children attended church with Marie and Tsu-la

.

Each Sunday when they arrived at the church, they made their way to Michael and Little Fawn would jump into Michael's arms and sit in his lap during the service. Michael had grown close to the child.

Little Gloria sat contentedly with her mother, while Gv-nv-ge Yo-na was not happy unless he sat in Tsu-la's lap. The man felt a special closeness and bond with the boy, having helped bring him into the world. He continually marveled at the child's likeness to Running Deer.

CHAPTER THIRTY-SEVEN

The Invitation

A few days later, after supper was over, White Feather joined Marie and Tsu-la on the porch. The children were asleep and she felt lonely, so when Marie called her to come sit with them she had not hesitated.

The three friends sat quietly gazing at the twilight sky, commenting on the bright star formations and then becoming silent.

Tsu-la interrupted the quietness unexpectedly. "White Feather," he began seriously, "there's something we would like to talk to you about."

White Feather's heart began to race and her breath quickened, fearing that her friends might have discovered her plans to leave their home and go back to the mountains. She knew that Tsu-la and Marie would not approve because they assumed that she would remain in the new territory and begin a new life here.

"Marie and I feel that you should get away from the house occasionally." Tsu-la began. "You never leave here, not even to go into town with us. We want you to know our friends, and make new friends for yourself."

White Feather breathed a sigh of relief. Before Tsu-la could continue she spoke, "I am happy here."

"White Feather, you must have a life again. You can't hide yourself away forever," said Tsu-la.

"And, dear, you are young," joined Marie. "You need to begin building a new life for yourself now."

White Feather said nothing, her eyes downward.

"There are so many fine young people in our town about your age, both white and Indian, and we'd like for you to meet some of them," Tsu-la said.

"I am happy staying here with the children," she said.

"And we are glad, but White Feather, you need friends...friends your own age."

"And there are some respected young men in town too, I must add," chuckled Tsu-la. "Many of them are anxious to meet you."

"How can Tsu-la say that?" she thought. "No man could ever match Running Deer." But her spoken words belied her thoughts.

"Tsu-la, you are very kind but I like staying here with the children...keeping house for you and Marie."

"And we appreciate it, darling," Marie said sweetly, placing her hand on White Feather's arm, "but we want you to have more from life than minding children and housekeeping," Marie paused, then continued. "Our town is having a picnic next Sunday after church and we want you to go with us."

Without waiting for White Feather to answer, Tsu-la quickly added to the invitation.

"Gv-nv-ge Yo-na and Little Fawn will love playing with all the children who will be there, White Feather. You can't keep them penned up here forever. Think of them," he continued gently, "and yourself."

"Please go, White Feather," pleaded Marie. "Please say that you'll go. You will have fun," Marie smiled.

"I'll think about it," White Feather said, turning to look at Marie.

Not wanting to push for an immediate answer, Tsu-la and Marie became silent.

White Feather mulled over the idea. Her friends had asked so little of her and they had done so much for her children. They just wanted her to go to a picnic. Maybe she should go, if only to please them. "But," she argued with herself, "Captain Howard will be there most probably." No, she didn't want to face him again. But, then again, she had to admit to herself that she did miss having friends her own age. Maybe she would go. She would avoid the captain if he came to the picnic. She suddenly realized that she did find herself lonely sometimes; actually, lonely more times than she cared to remember.

"I will go with you," she spoke unexpectedly.

"Wonderful," Marie said happily. "I know you will have a good time."

"Good," added Tsu-la, smiling.

"I'll see you in the morning," White Feather said quietly and got up to go into the house.

As she prepared for bed, White Feather dwelled on other thoughts. Marie's baby would be born in a few months and then she would begin her plans for going home.

"We will go back!" she said aloud, and then she added sadly, "But, now, without Running Deer."

Her hand automatically touched the gold nugget hidden over her heart. She closed her eyes and a vision of Running Deer appeared and lifted her spirits. He wanted her to go home. She would not be lonely there or lack for friends either.

She knew that the Cherokee who hid from the soldiers in the mountains would be there to welcome her. But most of all, the beautiful mountains would be there...the river, the streams, the flowers, and her future.

CHAPTER THIRTY-EIGHT

Going to the Water Again

White Feather had to admit that she was enjoying the picnic with Tsu-la and his family. She had met many new people who were very friendly and made her feel welcome at the outing. Some of the young men were even attentive to her. Cordial and polite, White Feather acknowledged their interest without encouraging their overtures.

Just as she had expected, Michael came to the picnic. He showed up alone, which surprised White Feather since she thought she would see him in the company of a young lady. She had observed that he seemed to be very popular with the unattached females, but he didn't appear to be interested in any of them. She was relieved that Michael had only spoken to her and did not try to start a conversation.

The picnic meal had lasted long and White Feather felt tired from the emotional strain of meeting so many people for the first time. She remembered with a sudden gladness the gatherings her people enjoyed back in the mountains and the joy she had shared with her Indian friends.

After everyone had finished eating Tsu-la joined a group of his male friends sitting in the shade of a oak tree and Marie had stretched out beside the children where they lay napping on a blanket. White Feather sat beside Marie and the children for a while and then became restless as the day stretched into the lazy afternoon. Soon she became bored with nothing to do.

Suddenly she thought of the lake surrounded by tall green trees that they had passed on the road leading to the picnic grounds. The sight of it had made White Feather remember how much she missed swimming in the cool river of her mountain home. She loved swimming; just the thought of the feel of the water on her body made her want to investigate the lake.

Glancing at the children sleeping soundly, she turned to look over the picnic area and she saw that everyone was either resting or visiting with friends. No one was looking. No one would really miss her if she slipped away for a short time, but perhaps she should tell Marie. She wouldn't want Marie or Tsu-la to be worried if they missed her.

"Marie, if you don't mind, while the children are sleeping, I think I will take a walk, maybe down to the lake," she said rising to her feet.

"Of course, dear," Marie answered drowsily. "But, please, don't be gone too long. We will be starting for home soon. The children will sleep for a while, I'm sure." She looked over at the children and smiled. "They're so tired from playing with their friends," she added, stroking Gv-nv-ge Yo-na's long hair.

White Feather had begged off participating in a ball game with some of the young people after lunch, and now she walked past the game in progress and headed for the road leading to the lake. She saw Michael playing in the game and he waved to her when she reached the road. She did not acknowledge his greeting, not wanting to encourage him. A moment later, she admonished herself.

"He is a nice person and so kind. I am ashamed

to behave this way," she scolded herself.

She looked back to return his wave but he had returned his attention to the game.

The lake, sparkling in the sunlight came into view when she turned the sharp bend in the road. She moved faster as she approached the water. The lake looked inviting and there was no one around. When she neared the water, she found herself running. At the water's edge, she paused for a moment, then headed quickly for the wooded area beside the lake. Rapidly shedding her shoes and clothes, she tossed them on the ground behind a large clump of bushes. She could barely wait to feel the cool water on her body as she waded, naked, into the the lake.

Closing her eyes, White Feather smiled in enjoyment while she swam and splashed, pretending that she was back home in the mountain river. She floated on her back with her eyes closed and thought of Running Deer and the wonderful times they had spent swimming together in the river by their cabin. Going to the water would be one of the first things she planned to do when she returned to the Cherokee lands. She felt she could have stayed in the water for the remainder of the day, but she knew that she must get back. She should not worry Marie.

Reluctantly she began to wade slowly out of the water. Almost to the water's edge of the lake, a sudden noise halted her. It was a horse! The sound came closer and closer. Quickly, she ran out of the water, gathered her shoes and clothes and ran into the woods, hoping to conceal herself until the horse and rider passed by. She stopped near a tall bush and hurriedly wrapped her dress around her bare body and realized that one of her shoes was missing. Cautiously peering out from between leaves of the bush hiding her, she saw the shoe lying in full view. There was no time to retrieve it. She quickly took her hand away from the foliage and crouched lower behind the bush, hoping that she would not be seen. Her heart pounded with fear. During the brief moment she peered out from her hiding place, she had caught sight of the approaching rider. The rider was a man she had not seen at the picnic, she was sure. He was unshaven and wore dirty clothes. He held a whiskey bottle in one hand as he reeled from side to side in his saddle.

"Whoa, old boy," a slurred voice boomed out, "les' get you a little drink."

Carefully White Feather peered out again. The rider slid from his horse, paused and turned the bottle up to his mouth and drank the remainder of the whiskey. He threw the empty bottle on the ground and swaying, walked toward the water leading the horse behind him.

"Come'on, old boy."

When he neared the lake he saw White Feather's shoe lying on the ground.

"Well, lookee here," he said as he picked up the shoe. "Looks like some filly's done went and lost her shoe."

White Feather froze as the rider turned and scanned the nearby woods with his beady eyes. Looking back at the lake's edge he saw the wet tracks on the sand leading out of the water. "And she ain't been gone long either," he added, following the wet trail with his eyes.

"Les' just see where these tracks go." Reeling in drunkenness the man followed the trail. "Les' just see what's in these here bushes," he said.

White Feather was paralyzed with fear as the man approached her hiding place. She was sure that he could hear the wild pounding of her heart.

Suddenly the foliage parted in front of her. Gasping, she shrank back. The red- faced man leered at her, then laughed loudly. He reached out, grabbed her roughly by the arm and pulled her up from her crouched position.

White Feather screamed and wrenched her arm loose from his grip. She pulled her dress closely about her body and started running.

He let out a raucous laugh and began staggering after White Feather.

She was a fast runner but her bare feet on the rough ground slowed her pace enough so that the man finally caught up with her.

He snatched her roughly from behind and swung her around to face him.

"Well, I done found myself a little Injun," he laughed, pulling White Feather so close that she thought she would be ill from the smell of his sour whiskey breath.

She tried to free her arm from his vice-like grip.

He snapped her arm back with a force that sent pain surging, She screamed and begged to be released while the man laughed at her.

"Ain't you a frisky little thing?" he sneered, showing an almost toothless grin.

His beefy hand fumbled at her clothes as he attempted to loosen the dress from about her body.

Catching the man off guard she jerked her throbbing arm loose from his hold and blindly ran again, this time escaping into bramble bushes that tore long scratches down her arms and legs. The pain slowed her pace. The man caught her once again, Turning her to face him, his long fingernails raked down her shoulder, leaving a deep wound. She felt the warm blood.

He pinned both her arms behind her back, bruising them with his uncaring hands. Sneering into her face he said in a low voice, "I like my women with a little spunk." Then he laughed harshly, shaking her roughly. He pulled the dress from around her body leaving White Feather standing unclothed before him.

"Now ain't you the pretty little Injun?" he said, running his free hand roughly across her breasts.

His gaze fell on the leather pouch hanging from her neck. His blurred eyes squinted and he leaned toward her to inspect it closer.

"What is this thing around your neck? One of them superstitious things you Injuns wear?"

White Feather's heart almost stopped at the mention of the pouch.

He reached toward her and she screamed, kicking him.   Her foot found its target and he yelled in pain as he released her to grab his crotch. She turned and ran.   He came after her with foul, angry words pouring from his mouth.   Before she could get away he grabbed her and pulled her to the ground.   He rolled her over on her back and slapped her across the face.

"Now you done gone and made me mad," he said angrily and hit her face again. "Real mad!"   And he struck her face with his fist.

White Feather struggled to free herself and each time she moved he hit her.

"You gonna be sorry for what you gone and done, girlie.   I ain't hurt so bad I can't take care of you, like it or not!" He laughed loudly and then struck her again. This blow hit her eye and just before the wave of darkness took her away, she saw him standing over her, fumbling to remove his trousers. The last thing she felt was his body as he fell across her.

CHAPTER THIRTY-NINE

Dark Bruises of Intent

Michael watched White Feather disappear down the road. The ball game ended and he became increasingly concerned as time went by and she had not returned. He thought of asking Marie about White Feather's whereabouts but Marie and the children were asleep; he did not wish to disturb them. And he didn't want to ask Tsu-la. He would be alarmed for sure.

Tsu-la had been talking to his friends with his back toward the road, so he wasn't even aware that White Feather had left.

Finally Michael could not wait any longer. He decided to go search for her, fearing that she might have wandered off into the unfamiliar woods and could not find her way back.

He had brought his buckboard with him to the picnic. He hitched his horse to the wagon, quickly got into the wagon, and guided him out onto the road to begin his search for White Feather.

Slapping the reigns, Michael hurried his horse down the road. When he neared the lake he thought

he heard a scream. "What was that?" The sound
jarred him.

When he heard the second scream, Michael
snapped the reins against the horse's sides and the
wagon surged forward.

Approaching the lake, he saw a horse standing
by the water with an empty saddle and then, he spied
the discarded whiskey bottle. He stopped the wagon,
leaped from it and ran into the woods following the
sound of the screams. He thrashed about among the
bushes and ran between the trees, but there was no
sign of White Feather. He continued running and calling her name, becoming more frantic each minute.

Suddenly, Michael's mad rush brought him
upon the drunken man standing over White Feather.
She was lying motionless. The man was so caught up
in his intent that he was not aware of Michael's presence.

Inflamed, Michael's usual calm temper disappeared. Anger trembled down his arms. If he had
been wearing a gun he would have killed the man.
Looking around for the nearest weapon, he picked up
a dead limb and swung with the power of his whole
being. The invader pitched forward and Michael hit
him again, this time striking him across the back.
The attacker never knew what hit him. Michael rolled
the man off White Feather's battered body and
stooped to gather her gently into his arms.

He rushed back to the buckboard cradling her
and swearing under his breath.

At the wagon he laid her in the back and
wrapped her limp form in a blanket. He smoothed her
long dark hair away from her face, fury setting his face
when he saw the swelling and the dark bruises on her
face.

For the moment the would-be rapist was forgotten and Michael's only thoughts were to get medical
help for White Feather. He knew that the town's only
doctor had left the picnic earlier to see an emergency
patient in his office and Michael prayed that he would

still be there. Glancing nervously at White Feather's unmoving body, he raced the horse down the road. Her face, swollen from the many blows she had received, had now grown almost unrecognizable.

Michael reached town in a cloud of dust. He stopped the horse in front of the doctor's office, relieved to see that his carriage sat in front of the building. Carefully lifting White Feather in his arms, he clenched his teeth and ran toward the doctor's office.

Michael burst into the room, shouting for the doctor.

Doc Lee was startled momentarily. He was alone in his office, cleaning up after dismissing his earlier patient. At the sight of Michael and White Feather he quickly rushed to them.

"What has happened to her? Put her here." he said, and then watched as Michael lay her carefully on the examining table.

In broken emotional words Michael attempted to relate what he had found happening in the woods. "Attacked...beaten...attempted rape. She's been beaten... attacked by a drunk."

Doctor Lee saw Michael's distraught condition and he knew that he could not perform his examination with Michael hovering over her.

"Son," the doctor said gently, placing a hand on Michael's shoulder, "you wait outside. I'll see to her."

"Take care of her, Doc," Michael stammered.

The angry man backed toward the door, and then in the silence of the waiting room, he found himself still trembling.

"Why?" thought Michael. "Why would a man hurt a woman so badly?" He hesitated and rubbed his eyes. He forced himself to walk out of the waiting room through the doorway into the air of the afternoon. He sat on the steps of the building, head bowed, emotionally exhausted.

When Marie arose from her nap she sat up, stretched and smiled down at the children still sleeping peacefully. She pushed hair away from Gloria's face, and then looked around for White Feather. She did not see the young woman anywhere. Had White Feather not come back? Keeping her eyes on the road, anticipating White Feather's return at any moment, Marie became disturbed, beginning to worry that something could have happened to her. The children awoke and began playing with their friends, so Marie quickly walked the short distance to where Tsu-la sat. She leaned down over his shoulder and whispered her concern for White Feather.

The news alarmed him also and he rose to his feet, excusing himself from the group and hurriedly went to his horse. He did not take time to saddle the animal; instead, mounted the horse and immediately rode off toward the lake while Marie returned to the children.

When Tsu-la neared the water he saw Michael turn his buckboard out onto the road leading toward town. In the shallow bed he saw a woman covered by a blanket. Fear stabbed at his heart. It had to be White Feather! He shouted and waved to Michael in an effort to stop his friend, but Michael did not slow down. He sped away, leaving a cloud of dust behind him.

Tsu-la prodded his horse to go faster in an attempt to catch up with Michael, but his friend had faded from sight around the bend.

Tsu-la jabbed his heels into the sides of his horse again in an effort to overtake Michael, but he had a head start and was moving so rapidly that Tsu-la could do nothing more than follow in the wake of his dust.

Jumping from his horse, Tsu-la ran to Michael and stood anxiously before him. "Where is White Feather? What is wrong?"

Michael did not answer.

"Michael!" his voice rose loudly, "What is wrong?"

"Some drunk hurt White Feather...beat her ...."

said Michael as he raised his face to Tsu-la.

"Will White Feather be all right?" Tsu-la asked.

"I don't know," responded Michael. "The doctor has told me nothing."

Tsu-la left Michael and bounded into the office to catch the doctor on his way through the waiting room toward the back. "How is she, Doc?"

"She's alive, but badly beaten. Don't worry, though...she'll live. Now, leave me to do my work, Tsu-la." The doctor continued his quick pace toward the backroom door.

As the man full of anger came out of the doctor's office, he headed toward his horse. "I'll kill the man who did this to White Feather," Tsu-la lashed out, stopping to face Michael. "Where is he?"

"I don't know," Michael replied. "I left him lying in the woods. My only thought was to get help for White Feather and deal with him later."

"He must be found and punished," retorted Tsu-la, his increasing anger rivaling Michael's. "I will find him after I take Marie and the children home. Believe me, I will find him. You stay here in case White Feather needs anything. I'll be back."

Tsu-la mounted, turned his horse, and sped away.

Watching Tsu-la's rapid departure, Michael could only think of how much the small woman lying in the bed inside had endured. Life just didn't seem to be fair to some.

CHAPTER FORTY

Waiting in a Deserted Town

Michael stared at the deserted street. The townspeople were all at the picnic. It seemed as if it had been an eternity since he left White Feather in the doctor's care. Pacing back and forth on the porch, he grew more anxious by the minute.

Finally, he sat back down on the steps and gazed at the setting sun, wondering how much longer he would have to wait. Suddenly, the doctor appeared in the door. Michael leaped to his feet, putting his trembling hand on the doctor's shoulder. Through anguished eyes he searched the doctor's face for answers.

"Doctor, is she de...." Michael could not say the word that had loomed in his mind all afternoon.

"Michael, come sit with me." The doctor pointed to the chairs on the small porch.

The elderly doctor sat down wearily and leaned back in his chair, closed his eyes for a moment, then motioned for Michael to join him.

Michael sat down, leaned toward the doctor and asked again, glancing toward the door. "Tell me, Doc."

"She'll be all right."

Michael's tired shoulders sagged as he breathed a sigh of relief.

"But she has been beaten. Her body has suffered much pain. Tell me what happened, Michael. Tell me how this girl received such brutal abuse."

Once again Michael related the scene he had discovered taking place when he found her. This time Michael was more coherent and the doctor understood more about the incident than Michael had been able to tell Tsu-la.

"Who was the man?"

"I don't know. I've never seen him before; at least I don't think so. His back was to me and I only glimpsed his face," explained Michael. "Doctor, please, can I see White Feather?"

"Not now, she is sleeping. The girl needs rest now. I have given her medication to help her." The doctor paused, looking at the man. "Go home, Michael. There is nothing you can do here now. She will sleep for hours. You can visit her later, perhaps tomorrow."

The doctor stood to go back inside and Michael rose from his chair.

"No, I will wait here," he responded. "Tsu-la left me here to care for her."

The sympathetic doctor patted Michael lightly on the shoulder and returned to his patient.

Michael dropped back down in the chair to wait.

CHAPTER FORTY-ONE

Man Found Dead

Tsu-la had ridden out of town with mixed emotions churning in his mind; worry for White Feather and anger for the man who had hurt her.

He thought of his dear friend, Running Deer. He knew that Running Deer would have killed anyone with his bare hands who brought harm to White Feather. Tsu-la's eyes clouded as he remembered the love the three of them had shared for each other during the times they had spent together back in the land of their ancestors. It seemed such a long time ago. So much had happened since then. He slowly moved his head from side to side remembering the bad times.

"The man will pay, Running Deer," Tsu-la vowed silently.

Returning to the lake, Tsu-la followed the trail made by the wagon wheels. He found no trace of the man or his horse. What he did find was White Feather's clothes and shoes scattered through the woods. He gently collected each piece and laid them across his arm with the thoughts of returning them to her, but he changed his mind. "She will probably not want to see these clothes," he thought. "I will take these home and bring new ones for her."

Tsu-la found the empty whiskey bottle and the fresh tracks of a horse in the soft sand. The tracks led away from the water and into the tall grass and onward toward the picnic area. Mounting his horse, Tsu-la followed the tracks but lost them when they faded into the thick underbrush.

"Marie! Marie and the children," he thought suddenly. He needed to go to them. "Marie must be worried sick about White Feather."

Riding toward the picnic site, he heard loud voices in the woods ahead of him. He raised himself to gain a better view and saw a group of young men he recognized who had been at the picnic.

He slowly halted his horse near the circle of men. "What has happened?" he called.

The men parted, revealing a man lying crumpled on the ground. "We were walking in the woods and found this man lying on the ground with his horse nearby. He is dead," said Malcolm, Marie's cousin.

"Dead!" said Tsu-la.

"Yes. He has a wound on the front of his head and we believe he hit his head on that low limb of this tree when it knocked him from his horse," answered one of the men.

"His neck is broken."

"Looks like he might have been drunk," said Malcolm.

"He was drinking, all right," stated a man in the crowd. "He smells awful."

Tsu-la dismounted and walked to the man on the ground. He stooped and peered closely into the man's face.

"This is White Feather's attacker," he thought. Anger flared through Tsu-la's body and he suppressed the desire to kick the man. He would love to kick him over and over, but it wouldn't accomplish anything nor would it undo the terrible pain the stranger had inflicted on White Feather.

"Who is he?" Tsu-la stood, turning toward Malcolm.

"None of us have ever seen him before," Malcolm replied. "He must have been a drifter passing through."

"Well, there's no need to take him to Doc Lee. Doc can't do him any good now," said another man standing nearby.

Tsu-la did not know the extent of the attack on White Feather. As he stood looking at the demise of the man, he simply made the decision to say nothing.

"Yeah. We'd better get him to the sheriff's office," added one of the men.

"I'll take him," Malcolm said.

"I need to take Marie and the children home," Tsu-la muttered. "Looks like you have this under control." He mounted his horse and rode away.

As Tsu-la arrived at the picnic grounds, he observed the people preparing to depart for their homes. Picnickers were placing their belongings in their wagons, commenting on the afternoon and bidding farewell to their friends. Tsu-la was glad none of them were aware of White Feather's attack or of the discovery of the dead man. No one knew of what had happened to White Feather.

Marie struggled to her feet when he appeared.

"Tsu-la, I have been worried sick! Where is White Feather? And Michael! Where is Michael? I looked for him...to send him to find you. I was so worried...."

"Shh-h-h. It's all right," Tsu-la said as he dismounted and put his hand on her arm. He smiled. "There is no need for you to worry. Michael found White Feather at the lake and now they are together."

"White Feather and Michael...together?"

"Yes," he smiled and nodded. Tsu-la hated the idea of deceiving Marie, but for the moment it was necessary. He wanted to spare her anguish over White Feather's condition until he had her safely home. Then he would tell her the truth.

Marie returned his smile with a deep sigh.

"Thank goodness, she is all right. Will wonders never cease? After all this time White Feather has been ignoring Michael, now they are together. This is wonderful."

Satisfied by Tsu-la's story, Marie folded the blanket and called the children. Tsu-la helped them into the wagon and climbed onto the seat, ready for the ride home.

He was relieved that Marie believed his story about White Feather and Michael, but now it occurred to him that there would be no one at home to be with her and the children when he returned to town. Pondering over the situation and what he should do about it he heard a familiar loud laugh nearby.

"Miss Annie," he thought. "I'll get Miss Annie."

"Marie," Tsu-la pulled up on the reins. "I must go speak to Miss Annie before we leave. I haven't spoken to her at all today."

Marie nodded to her husband, pleased that he thought well of her relative and she waited patiently for him in the wagon. She could not hear their words and thought it seemed a little strange that both their faces looked so serious while they talked, but the children distracted Marie and she turned to give them her attention.

Tsu-la returned to the wagon and tried to sound cheerful as they began their trip home.

CHAPTER FORTY-TWO

Attachment

The sun slowly disappeared as dusk covered the little town. Michael, pale and haggard, remained where Doc Lee had left him. Tsu-la had not returned. Michael wondered what had occurred after he left. Perhaps Tsu-la had found and actually killed the man. He could be sitting behind bars in jail for murder, but Michael had seen no one come into town. Had Tsu-la told Marie about White Feather? And White Feather! What was going on behind the closed door of the doctor's office? His mind raced...a protective feeling was rising within him. He could feel it. There was more to this than what he wanted to face at the moment.

The door opened behind him and the doctor appeared. Michael sprang to his feet.

"I thought I might find you still here," he said as he quietly closed the door behind him. "I made a pot of good strong coffee. I think we both need it...here, son, drink this." The old man smiled and handed him a cup.

Michael took the coffee and looked expectantly

toward the doctor and pleaded, "Could I see White Feather?"

"It's not a pretty sight," Doc said . "Her face is swollen badly."

"It doesn't matter. I only want her to know that someone is here with her." Setting the cup of coffee down on the porch, the anxious man stood.

"She probably won't realize that, Michael. She's slipping in and out of sleep from the medication I gave her to relieve the pain."

"I understand," Michael said, walking toward the door.

"Wait! You must not stay more than a moment. White Feather has suffered great trauma. You must not say or do anything to upset her," the doctor warned.

"I won't. I give you my word," Michael said and eased the door open.

"Not too long, Michael."

Passing through the patients' waiting room, Michael found White Feather lying on a cot with a sheet covering her. He came close and stood by her bed. He knew that she would look swollen but he was not prepared for what he saw.

Her face was a mass of cuts and bruises. Michael clenched his fists, then leaned over White Feather, whispering softly, "White Feather, I am here."

She did not move nor did she open her eyes. Michael felt helpless. He knew that she was sleeping and he kept his promise to the doctor. Reluctantly he backed out of the room.

Tsu-la had returned and was dismounting when Michael stepped onto the porch. He bounded up the steps.

"Michael, is she alive?" he inquired anxiously.

"Yes. Come sit," Michael said.

The doctor excused himself and went back inside to continue his vigil over White Feather.

Michael began. "Tsu-la, did you tell Marie what happened?"

"Yes."

"How is she taking it?"

"Better...when I left. She was very upset over White Feather. Miss Annie is with her and the children. When we put Marie to bed, she insisted that I come back here."

"The children?" He had completely forgotten that White Feather's children might be upset that their mother was not home with them.

"Miss Annie has agreed to stay and care for the children and help Marie until White Feather is well again. Now...about White Feather?"

Michael told him of the shocking sight of her swollen face. "That was all I saw. I don't know everything."

Tsu-la's face clouded and he leaned closer to Michael, lowering his voice, "Did the man...?"

"No," Michael said, "the doctor says he didn't. Fortunately I got there in time to stop him before he had a chance."

"Does White Feather know this?"

"I don't know. She has not been awake. The doctor says she has not spoken."

The two men sat in silence for a moment.

"Tsu-la, did you find the man who did this?"

"Yes." he said, and then he told Michael all that had happened since leaving the town earlier. He was sure that the dead man was the person who attacked White Feather in the woods. "I'm going to the sheriff's office in the morning to talk to him. Will you come?"

Michael did not answer for a moment, lost in thought. Finally he spoke, "Yes, but I do not want the sheriff speaking to White Feather until she has fully recovered from the attack." Michael paused thoughtfully for a moment and then continued, "Who knows about what happened?"

"You mean what happened to White Feather?"

"Yes."

"Only you, Marie, Miss Annie, Doc Lee and myself," answered Tsu-la. "No one at the picnic knows, so...."

"So?"

"So, is it necessary, then, to tell the sheriff?" Tsu-la asked. "White Feather could be spared from answering questions if we did not tell him about the attack."

"I know we can keep this secret, but what about Doc and Miss Annie?" Michael paced the floor.

"Neither of them are gossips. They wouldn't talk if we asked them not to. The man's already been punished."

"But, I...." began Michael.

"You didn't kill him. He got up and rode his horse after you left him. He had a knot on his head all right! But you didn't kill him." Tsu-la paused, then continued. "No one has to know about White Feather."

"But what do we tell the children about their mother's absence?"

"We've told them that their mother hurt her arm and needs to stay at the doctor's office for a few days."

"Did that satisfy them?"

"Seems to have. Now, come on, Michael, let's go home and have something to eat. The doctor will take care of White Feather tonight."

"No. I want to stay."

"You can come back tomorrow, Michael."

"But I feel one of us needs to be here when she wakes up. I'll stay...you go on home."

Tsu-la shook his head slowly, recognizing that Michael was right; besides, he could see a new expression growing in his friend's eyes. He patted him on the shoulder before he went to his horse, settled himself on his steed and looked at Michael. "I will be back in the morning." He rode way with a smile on his face.

CHAPTER FORTY-THREE

A Reaction

During the night White Feather opened her eyes several times. She realized she was in a strange place. Then she saw a man asleep in a chair close to her bed. Low lamplight lit the room, but she did not recognize the old man. Fear seized her.

She raised her head, trying to get out of bed but searing pain caused her to cry out. She fell back on the bed.

Her cry awakened the doctor and he came to her bedside immediately.

"It's all right, White Feather," Doc said softly.

Still frightened, she tried to move again. Through the swollen slits of her eyes, her gaze darted around the room.

"Shhh...I'm your doctor. Stay quiet. You're all right."

The doctor's soothing soft voice began to calm her. She was too weak to attempt to rise again and her body relaxed as she drifted back to sleep.

The tired doctor returned to his chair and then, he too, immediately closed his eyes to sleep.

When the sun rose, White Feather opened her eyes once more.

"How are you feeling this morning, White Feather?"

Doc Lee sat across the room with his back to his desk drinking a cup of coffee. He smiled.

White Feather tried to respond but her swollen lips could not form the words. Her face and body ached. She hurt everywhere. "How did I get here?" she wondered silently, "and where are Marie and Tsula and my children?"

Doc Lee pulled his chair close to the side of the cot and slowly told White Feather what had happened the previous day. He explained how Michael had halted the attack and brought her to his office for medical care.

"Michael?" she thought, "Michael? Who is Michael?" And then she remembered, "Captain Howard...he brought me here?"

Her thoughts were interrupted by the doctor's continued explanation. "Michael has been here all night, sitting on the porch, worried sick about you."

"Michael?" she thought again. "All night? He seems to always be near when I need someone."

"I just took him a cup of coffee and he's very anxious to see you. Would you like for him to come in?"

White Feather slowly moved her head from side to side and whispered, "No."

"Are you sure you don't want to see him? He has been here all night."

Without waiting for a response, he walked to the door and called, "Michael, she's awake!" He stepped outside and left the door open.

At the sound of Michael's approaching footsteps White Feather closed her eyes, pretending to be asleep. She did not want to talk to him.

Michael stood and looked down at White Feather and grimaced at the now yellowing bruises of her delicate face. "Hello, White Feather," he said.

When she did not respond, Michael spoke again,

"How are you feeling today?"

Still no response.

"You're going to be well again, you know. You really are. You're strong. I've seen you overcome troubles before. You will survive this too."

She did not respond but she was hearing his words.

"I'll let you rest...but I'll not leave you," Michael said softly and started to leave the room.

As his hand touched the doorknob, he heard a weak voice behind him.

"Captain Howard...."

Swinging around, he hurried back to her side. "Did you call me?" he said.

"Thank you, I...," and her voice stopped.

"You're tired, White Feather. I'll go see about my business and be right back."

She opened her eyes slightly, then closed them and whispered, "Yes, Michael."

At the sound of his given name, his heart grew warm in his chest. A smile began there and moved to his lips. He opened the door and let himself out.

CHAPTER FORTY-FOUR

Declaration of Apology

At the doctor's insistence Michael left for a short time during the morning to change his clothes and open his business. By noon he was back to see White Feather.

Tsu-la had come while Michael was gone; he was relieved when the doctor told him that she was regaining her strength.

"My children?" she had murmured.

"They're in good hands. Miss Annie is at my house. She's caring for Marie and the children."

"That is good," she whispered.

"You will be strong enough to go home soon. I promise that Miss Annie will not take your job," he laughed.

White Feather tried to smile. He had said home.... Home. If he only knew. Oh, how she longed to see the Cherokee lands again. The thought filled her with warmth and she drifted off again with dreams of the blue-green mountains in the distance.

Mrs. Shepherd, Doc Lee's nurse, who had arrived earlier, entered the room, passing Tsu-la on his way out. She smoothed the covers, brushed the hair out of White Feather's face and then sat down beside her patient.

A while later, Michael peered into the room.

Almost as though she knew he was coming, White Feather opened her eyes.

"I hope you are feeling better this afternoon, White Feather," Michael began.

Mrs. Shepherd rose from her chair, nodded at Michael and slipped out of the room.

Michael walked to the side of the bed, smiled down at White Feather, but did not speak.

"Thank you, Michael," she managed to get out.

He said nothing in return, waiting for her to continue.

"Michael, I am sorry."

"Sorry? You have nothing to be sorry about."

"Yes, I have been....I'm sorry for the unkind way I have treated you."

"I understand, White Feather."

"No, you don't. You are a good man and I have treated you badly."

"It's all right," he said.

"No. I am ashamed. I have behaved badly."

The room was quiet. The sound of the clock ticking on the doctor's desk stabbed through the silence. White Feather looked away from Michael and whispered, "Why are you so good to me after the way I have behaved?"

Michael did not answer.

"Why?" she insisted.

"With all you've been through, you just need a friend."

White Feather looked at Michael from the corners of her eyes. He was sincere; she could feel his truth. An incredulous emotion swelled within her. "Well," she thought, "maybe we can be friends."

CHAPTER FORTY-FIVE

A Wise Old Doctor

Under the constant care of Doc and Mrs. Shepherd, White Feather began to improve, growing stronger each day. She even felt comfortable and relaxed with the doctor and his nurse.

White Feather had grown to admire Mrs. Shepherd, happily surprised that she was a Creek Indian. A child of one of the old settlers who arrived in the territory, Mrs. Shepherd had grown up and lived in the same place she was born. A widow now with no children, she was very devoted to Doctor Lee and his work. Townspeople thought that she and the doctor, a widower, would eventually get married. White Feather trusted Mrs. Shepherd as she did Doc Lee.

The two women had become close friends during White Feather's recovery. White Feather found her to be a sympathetic listener when she told her of the beauty she left behind in the land of her ancestors. Several times Mrs. Shepherd had questioned White Feather about the walk to the west, but White Feather would escape answering by pretending to be asleep.

She had no desire to remember the journey. She wanted to erase it from her mind and think only of returning to her homeland.

During the first day as White Feather slipped in and out of consciousness, she often dreamed of her home. In one dream she and Running Deer were laughing and running through the woods toward the river. When they stopped by the water's edge and turned to look into each other's faces she reached out to touch Running Deer's cheek. She called out his name, and then suddenly awoke briefly, only to fall unhappily back into a troubled sleep.

She had other dreams also. In one she remembered she was standing amid the mountains while she turned around in slow circles, arms outstretched, repeating over and over, "I am home! I am home! I am home!"

Another time she dreamed of Little Fawn and Gv-nv-ge Yo-na. They were lying in her arms close to her heart.

When she lay awake, her thoughts would turn to Captain Howard. She owed him so much. He had always been kind to her...on the walk...in Tsu-la's home. And now he had come to her rescue in the woods. She must be nicer to him.

Well, at least she could call him Michael...this seemed to please him.

Michael returned to visit her several times during the week, each time wearing a big smile. During his visits he never mentioned the man who had hurt her. She wondered if the man had been found, but she never asked.

On the fifth day White Feather's facial wounds were slowly disappearing, but her arm remained in a sling. The arm had been severely sprained, but she would regain the use of it, Doc Lee had assured her.

As White Feather lay in bed, she touched the small leather pouch around her neck and absently wondered why the doctor had not removed it during his examination when she was brought to his office.

Early in the afternoon Tsu-la and Michael arrived together to visit White Feather. Knowing that her condition had improved and she was stronger now, they felt that the time had come when they should discuss the events of the afternoon at the picnic.

Doc Lee and Mrs. Shepherd joined the men and they all sat down near White Feather's bed.

Mrs. Shepherd put pillows under White Feather's head and propped her up to a sitting position.

While Tsu-la and Michael each took turns relating the events that had taken place, White Feather's facial expression never changed, not even when Michael told her of the attacker's death.

Now Doc Lee was speaking, "White Feather, no one has to know what happened to you unless you choose to tell them."

"Marie and Miss Annie feel this way, too," added Tsu-la.

"No one has to know, dear. Doc Lee and I will never speak of it to anyone," said Mrs. Shepherd.

White Feather stared straight ahead, not seeing anything in front of her, but listening to their words.

"We only want what's best for you. The man can never harm you again. He is dead."

"I choose to forget the man and what he did to me, but there is something I will never forget," she said as her gaze turned toward Michael.

Tsu-la leaned forward in his chair, closely studying White Feather's face. "What is it," he asked in earnest.

"I can never forget how all of you have helped me. Thank you," she said softly, "and Michael, thank you for saving me. I will always be grateful."

"You are very welcome," he answered.

The old doctor, a romantic at heart, turned to Mrs. Shepherd and chuckled softly. He knew that these two young people were meant to be together. He could feel it .

CHAPTER FORTY-SIX

A Smile

By the seventh morning White Feather could not stand it any longer. She had to see her children. The young Cherokee woman pulled herself out of bed, bathed and then ate a big breakfast with Mrs. Shepherd at the small table by the fireplace. She walked about in the room, delighted that her legs felt strong again. She dressed herself in the new shoes and clothes Tsu-la had brought to her and she sat down to wait for the doctor.

When Doc arrived he greeted Mrs. Shepherd and then approached White Feather with a broad smile on his face.

"Now, don't you look nice," he said. "Well, young lady, I think that you are about ready to go home." He leaned over to examine the wounds on her face. "No bad scars left except the cut over your eye and these bruises are fading," he said, gently touching her face. "Keep your arm in the sling for a while longer until it is strong again."

There was knock at the door. Michael's head appeared. "May I come in?" he asked.

"Come on in. White Feather will be leaving us today," Doc said, patting his patient on the shoulder, then adding, "Mrs. Shepherd and I will miss her."

"I thought that you might be leaving this morning," Michael said, winking at the doctor for telling him the day before. "I brought my buckboard and I'd be happy to escort you home, m'lady," he teased, bowing low to White Feather. "I'll be waiting outside."

"I'll be there soon," she called to the retreating man.

Smiling at Doc Lee and Mrs. Shepherd, she thanked them for the care they had given her. The three of them walked to the porch together. "I will bring money to you soon, Doc, for payment for my care," she said, turning to the doctor.

"That's not necessary," Doc responded quietly.

"Yes, it is."

Michael met them on the porch. Taking White Feather's arm, he led her down the steps.

"Yep," the doctor whispered to Mrs. Shepherd, "those two are in love and they don't even know it."

Mrs. Shepherd chuckled and agreed as she and the doctor turned and disappeared into the office.

Before White Feather and Michael reached the wagon he paused and said, "White Feather, you've never been in town before, have you?"

"Once, to get Sa-lo-li."

"Do you feel strong enough for a short walk before we leave? It's a right nice day."

As anxious as she was to go to her children, she still agreed, thinking that this might be a good opportunity to find a place to sell her nugget. She would need to purchase supplies for her return trip to the mountains and she could make mental notes of the locations of the livery stables and stores where she could purchase clothes and food supplies. This was information she would need. She looked in each store they passed noting the wares they sold, disappointed that she did not see an establishment where she could sell the nugget. Who could she ask? Certainly not Marie or Tsu-la. They had no idea that she was plan-

ning to return to her home, and she did not want to
tell them for fear that they would try to stop her.
Could she ask Michael? No, definitely not Michael.
But who?

The couple strolled leisurely along the street
enjoying the warm sunshine while Michael talked constantly, pointing out and naming the places they saw.
People were beginning to come into town and when
they passed, Michael spoke friendly greetings to them,
but White Feather looked down and said nothing, not
wanting people to see her bruised face.

Michael slowed their pace and leaned close to
whisper in White Feather's ear. "Here comes Mrs.
Curtis, the town gossip. Don't let her upset you.
She's really a very nice person but she's very inquisi-
tive and the local news carrier, I'm afraid," he smiled.

White Feather glanced at the approaching
woman and looked down quickly.

"Mrs. Curtis," Michael said, as the three paused,
facing each other. "How are you today?"

"Good morning, Michael. I'm fine," she responded while her eyes traveled over White Feather. "And
you?"

"Very well, thank you. I'd like you to meet my
friend, White Feather," he said cordially. "And, White
Feather, this is Mrs. Curtis."

The younger woman nodded to the older woman
but did not hold up her head to look at her.

"White Feather, what happened to your arm,
dear?"

"She had a most unpleasant fall, Mrs. Curtis."
Michael jumped in. "She slipped and fell."

Mrs. Curtis's eyebrows went up as if to question
Michael's explanation while she tried to see White
Feather's face.

Michael rushed on, "We've just come from Doc
Lee's office."

"Tsk...tsk...and you hurt your face too, didn't
you?" she asked.

White Feather's heart was racing and she was
nearing panic from the meddling woman's questions,

but she made no response.

When White Feather did not answer, Mrs. Curtis rushed on.

"Where do you live, White Feather? Have you been here long? Were you on that awful Indian march from the east? You are Indian, aren't you?"

Ignoring the busybody's questions Michael gently guided White Feather past the woman and looking back over his shoulder, he called to her, "Good day, Mrs. Curtis, nice to see you."

Mrs. Curtis stood, mouth gaping while she watched White Feather and Michael quickly turn the corner and disappear. "Oh, of all the nerve!" she sputtered aloud, turning in a huff and proceeding down the street.

Michael laughed and White Feather couldn't help but smile at her escort.

The young man had waited so long to see her smile. It was beautiful; just as he had imagined it would be. He, himself, then smiled wide and helped her into the buckboard.

CHAPTER FORTY-SEVEN

Love Loses

Michael came to Tsu-la's house almost every night to visit White Feather after she left Doc Lee's office. White Feather was friendly to Michael now and they were comfortable with each other. She felt that she owed her life to him. Sometimes she shuddered to think what could have happened to her in the woods if Michael had not cared enough to go in search for her. She would always be grateful to him for saving her life. And she was surprised to realize that she did not always think of the march now when she saw him.

Miss Annie had returned to her home, and White Feather was again in charge of caring for Marie and the children. Everything seemed normal.

One warm evening, near twilight, about two weeks after White Feather had returned to Tsu-la's house, Marie had gone to bed early along with the children. Tsu-la was working late at the store so White Feather sat alone on the porch slowly rocking and dreaming of home.

She heard the sound of an approaching horse,

and looking up, she saw Michael riding toward the house. He stopped in front of the porch, dismounted and tied the reigns to a nearby tree.

"Good evening, m'lady. And how are you" he teased, approaching the porch.

"I'm fine, sir. And you?" she teased back.

"Fine, but I need the company of a lovely lady," he said, walking up the steps.

"Michael, I am sure that you have no trouble finding one of those admiring ladies who attended the picnic to keep you company."

"Not interested," he said, surprised that she had noticed him talking to the ladies at the outing. "Are you busy this evening?"

"No."

"Well, may I sit down?"

White Feather laughed and motioned to the empty chair beside her. "Of course."

He sat and inquired about the family. She informed him of everyone's whereabouts.

"So you are alone?" Michael asked.

"Well, yes, at least out here on the porch," she laughed.

"Good. I want to talk to you alone, without any interruptions."

"Oh?" She stopped rocking and looked at him.

"Yes. White Feather, there's something I want to say to you."

He paused, then continued seriously. "Do you remember the first night I visited you in Doc Lee's office after you were attacked?"

"I think so, but I slept much of the time from the medicine Doc gave me."

"Yes, I know, but do you remember I was there the first night and every night thereafter?"

Silence.

"White Feather, I realized my feelings then...," he said, not waiting for her to reply. "I've waited until you were well and strong again but now I want to tell you."

Silence.

He reached out and took her hand.

She flinched slightly at his touch and continued to stare out at the starry night.

"White Feather, look at me."

Slowly she turned and gazed downward.

"White Feather, I think I love you."

White Feather caught her breath. "Michael, you must not say such a thing. You don't know what you are saying."

He interrupted. "Yes, I do," he said huskily.

"No, in that big house, you are just lonely," she said pulling her hand away from him.

"I am not lonely."

"Yes, you are!"

"No, White Feather. I can have other companionship...it is you I want."

Silence.

"White Feather...."

She stopped his words, glanced at his face, and then again dropped her eyes. "Michael, I love you as a friend, a friend who saved my life, but...."

"But what...can't we be more than friends?"

White Feather stood slowly and walked to the edge of the porch and gazed at the full yellow moon now rising over the trees in front of the house.

Michael followed her, reached out and turned her to face him, sudden emotion causing him to hesitate. Never in his life had he felt this way. He wanted to pour his heart out to her. "I need you to care for me, White Feather," he finally got out.

"Mi...."

"White Feather, do you care for me at all?"

"Yes, I do. You are a fine respectable man. There are women who would be pleased and proud to be your wife," she said softly and turned away.

"But what about you?"

"I can't, Michael."

"Won't you try?"

"I can't."

"Tell me why not. Why not?"

"I have a love, Michael, and nothing can separate me from that love."

"Running Deer is not coming back, White Feather."

"It is not Running Deer. He was my dear love but he is gone. I know that."

"Well, who is it? "

Silence. White Feather could not give Michael an answer. All she could do was stare into the night.

Desperation filled the man who had suddenly realized the depth of his feelings for this Cherokee woman. Immediately, it came into his mind that he must not let her get away. With trepidation, Michael gathered White Feather into his arms and then gained enough courage to slowly lower his lips to hers.

White Feather could deny her feelings no longer, and responded to Michael's embrace. When the kiss ended, she laid her head on his chest and whispered, "I do love you, Michael."

Warmth shot through Michael's body as his heart pounded loudly in his ears. "You love me?" he said incredulously.

"Yes."

With arms of steel he drew her closer still and reveled in this newness of hope.

Abruptly she pulled away, turned and ran into the house, closing the door behind her. The flood of tears began as she leaned against the door. The realization of her love for Michael had burst forth so naturally that it had frightened her. She could never stay here in the west for the rest of her life even for Michael. Her love of home knew no bounds and could never be replaced. Besides, she had promised Running Deer....

She crawled into bed and cried silently throughout the night. So many thoughts raced through her mind that she experienced very little rest.

Always before her thoughts of going home brought happy restful sleep to White Feather, but now, they would not soothe her. She could not marry Michael and stay here. True, she would have a comfortable life with him. She knew that he would be a good husband and father for the children.

Since the day she had left the little cabin by the river she had vowed that she would return...someday.

The love for a man must never interfere.

CHAPTER FORTY-EIGHT

The Perplexed Tsu-la

Michael stood dazed in shock at the words White Feather had suddenly spoken to him. She had declared her love and then left abruptly. He had waited, thinking that she would return to the porch and explain what she meant. She had said she loved another. Who? He stood staring at the closed door for a long time anticipating her return, waiting for an explanation.

When he saw the light in her room go out he realized that she was not returning. Only the small glow from a lamp remained in the front room of the house, left for Tsu-la's return.

The anguished man sat on the porch steps, staring ahead, seeing nothing. This is how Tsu-la found him a while later when he returned from his store.

"Michael? What are you doing here alone on the porch? Is something wrong?" he asked anxiously glancing at the darkened house as he dismounted.

"Tsu-la...."

"What?" Tsu-la asked, approaching Michael.

"White Feather loves me," he said, sadly.

"She what?"

Michael nodded his head. "She told me."

"My friend," Tsu-la said brightly. "We all know that. She's the only one who hasn't known it," Tsu-la laughed, slapping his friend on the shoulder. Relieved that there was nothing wrong, he sat on the step beside Michael.

"But she won't marry me."

"Won't marry you?"

"No," Michael said sadly.

"Well, why not?"

Michael paused and then said, "There's someone else."

"How can there be someone else? She's not talking about...."

"No, it's not Running Deer. We talked about that."

"Well, then who?" Tsu-la was clearly puzzled.

"I don't know. Was there someone else back in the east?"

"No...no. White Feather never even looked at another man. She was very devoted to Running Deer."

Michael put his head in his hands and leaned over, his elbows on his knees. "And you know what's strange, Tsu-la?" He raised his head and looked at his friend. "I heard her crying after she went into the house."

The perplexed Tsu-la said nothing, trying to sort out all he had heard from Michael.

"My friend, I do not know what to make of all of this. You love White Feather. White Feather loves you, but she loves someone else too?"

"Yes," Michael nodded his head. "Who does she love? I have no idea. I'm going home but I will be back tomorrow and see if she will tell me." He rose to his feet, stepped quickly to the ground, then mounted his horse and rode away.

CHAPTER FORTY-NINE

The Unrelenting White Feather

Unexpectedly Marie's baby arrived, born three days after Michael's declaration of love, surprising everyone by his early arrival. The baby was the image of Tsu-la.

Ecstatic over the birth of his son, Tsu-la doted on the infant.

Each day Marie regained some of her strength. Soon she would be able to care for her children and take charge of the house by herself.

White Feather had waited eagerly for the time to arrive when she could leave and now the time was at hand. Even though Michael had almost insisted, she remained true to her instincts not to tell anyone of her plans. There were times when she was alone and tears would form in her eyes at the thought of leaving him. Hating deception, White Feather knew it would be difficult and wondered how to tell him when the time to leave arrived.

With no idea what lay ahead of her when she left with her children to face the unknown alone, she did know that her people were survivors. They had proved themselves to those who walked the trail with them. They...she...knew how to adjust. Only twenty-three years old, but life had taught her well. Now she felt the strength growing. She would not be afraid.

CHAPTER FIFTY

Your Secret is Safe With Me

White Feather found no place to sell the nugget. The only money she could glean came from her basket sales. What she needed was money for supplies.

White Feather had been unusually quiet all afternoon and Marie had noticed. She suggested that White Feather take a walk in the woods, thinking that she needed some time alone away from the active noisy children.

Welcoming the invitation White Feather left the house and walked to a nearby shaded area. She sat down by a tree trunk, leaning back on it to enjoy the quiet stillness.

Running Deer entered her mind and she whispered out loud, "Running Deer, I am trying...trying to take our children home, but I do not know what to do with the nugget. If you were only here...."

Her words had barely escaped her lips when the face of Doc Lee flashed across her mind. She raised her head, her dark eyes sparkling.

"Doc Lee!" she said. "Why have I not thought of him? He will know how to change the gold for money! He will help me!"

Somehow she knew that Doc Lee would understand. And Mrs. Shepherd would understand, too. Both of them knew of the deep love she had for her mountain home. Surely they would understand and help her without revealing her plan.

She rose quickly and started back to the house, lighthearted. By the time the house came into view, however, worry had once again settled on her shoulders. What would Tsu-la and Marie think, knowing that she wanted to see the doctor who had dismissed her as a patient? How could she see Doc without anyone knowing about it? She would have to work it all out.

White Feather did not have to wait long for an answer.

Three days later, just before daybreak, Gv-nv-ge Yo-na woke her with his crying, his body burning. Tsu-la awoke also and he came immediately to White Feather's room.

"He is hot with fever." said Tsu-la. "We must take him to Doc Lee." Without hesitation he returned to his room, dressed, and then went outside to hitch up the wagon.

White Feather dressed quickly and shortly the three of them were in the buckboard. Tsu-la raced the horse and wagon into town just as the sun rose on the horizon.

Doc Lee had arrived early at his office and was sitting on the porch enjoying a cup of coffee when Tsu-la pulled the buckboard up in front of the building, a cloud of dust following closely behind. Doc stood. When he saw White Feather's worried face and Gv-nv-ge Yo-na in her arms he motioned for her to follow him inside.

After Doc examined the child he explained to White Feather that Gv-nv-ge Yo-na's throat was inflamed. He gave him medication to bring down the high fever, explaining that it was not serious and that

Gv-nv-ge Yo-na would be well again in a few days.

When Doc turned to leave the room, White Feather touched him lightly on the arm. "Doc," she whispered.

He looked back at White Feather. "He'll be fine. Just be sure to give him all of the medicine in the bottle." He smiled. "There's no need to worry."

"Yes, I know," she responded. "But I need to ask you something very personal and important to me."

"What is it?" he asked. "You seem worried."

"Please promise me that no one will know the words I speak to you," she began, then added quickly, "unless you tell Mrs. Shepherd. I know she can be trusted."

"Of course," assured the doctor. "You have my word. Now, dear, what is it?"

"I have a gold nugget," she began, touching the small pouch under her blouse.

"I saw the pouch when you were here after the attack," he said.

"You never said anything. Didn't you wonder about my having it?"

He smiled. "Yes."

White Feather then told the doctor the story about the nugget and how she had kept the secret from everyone, including Tsu-la.

"Do you want to leave here, White Feather?" he asked, then added, "and leave Michael?"

"Yes...no. Oh, Doc. It's so hard. I don't want to leave Michael but I don't think I can ever be completely happy again until I go back."

"To stay?"

"Yes," she said, nodding her head. "It is my home. Running Deer knew that I could never be satisfied and completely happy anywhere else." She hung her head and whispered softly, "But, now I love Michael too."

"Have you told Michael of your plans, or Tsu-la and Marie?"

"No," she whispered sadly, looking down and

moving her head slowly from side to side.

"Are you going to tell them?"

"I don't know...perhaps when the time comes for me to leave."

"I see."

She lifted her head. "Please, will you help me?"

"Of course. It will be our secret," the doctor assured White Feather, patting her hand. "What do you want me to do?"

"I need to know where to sell the nugget. I will need to buy supplies for the trip. Could you tell me where to find someone who would buy it from me? Do you know such a person?"

` "Yes. I think I do," he smiled. "Let me look at it more closely."

White Feather quickly slipped the leather cord from around her neck and took the nugget out. Handing it to the doctor she said, "It's quite heavy."

Doc looked at it closely, then walked to the window and examined it again in the sunlight. "Yes, it is," he replied. He turned around and looked at White Feather. "Can you leave it with me for a few days?"

"Of course," she replied, trusting the doctor completely.

"Are you sure that you want to sell it?"

"Yes."

"Tell Tsu-la that I will need to see Gv-nv-ge Yo-na again. Have him bring you and Gv-nv-ge Yo-na to my office day after tomorrow. I will be able to help you then."

White Feather smiled from her heart. "Thank you, Doctor. I knew that you would help me."

"Now, go, before Tsu-la becomes worried." He walked back to White Feather and took her arm and led her to the door. He paused and whispered, "Your secret is safe with me."

CHAPTER FIFTY-ONE

A Fair Price for the Nugget

Gv-nv-ge Yo-na improved almost immediately after taking the medicine, but White Feather insisted that Tsu-la take them back to Doc Lee's office. Tsu-la did not think it was necessary; however, he relented at White Feather's urging.

"White Feather," Tsu-la said. "Now that Marie is strong again you might want to have your own house. We could look for land after we see Doc Lee."

"Thank you, Tsu-la, but couldn't we do it some other time? I really need to get back and help Marie." She knew that Marie could manage without her, but it was a good excuse to put off moving into a house of her own.

"Yes, I suppose so. Well, here we are. I'll go over and check on things at the store while you are with Doc and then come back for you and Gv-nv-ge Yo-na."

"Fine," she said as Tsu-la helped her and Gv-nv-ge Yo-na out of the buckboard.

"Don't hurry," she tossed over her shoulder as Tsu-la drove away.

White Feather bounded up the steps and was met by Mrs. Shepherd when she entered the office. Mrs. Shepherd hugged her close and whispered in White Feather's ear, "I'm going to miss you."

Surprised by the words, White Feather pulled away and looked into Mrs. Shepherd's smiling face. From her expression, White Feather could tell that Doc had found someone who would buy the nugget.

"Can I see Doc now?" she said, feeling the warmth move over her body.

"Go right in," Mrs. Shepherd motioned to the door.

Doc was sitting at his desk, slumped over the papers strewn about, but he rose when White Feather entered with Gv-nv-ge Yo-na.

"Doc, did you...?"

"Just a minute, White Feather. Let's see how this big boy is doing," he said taking Gv-nv-ge Yo-na out of White Feather's arms and placing him on the examination table.

White Feather waited patiently while Doc examined her child.

When Doc finished, he called Mrs. Shepherd to come in and take Gv-nv-ge Yo-na out on the porch to entertain him while he spoke with White Feather.

As soon as Mrs. Shepherd closed the door White Feather began. "Doc, tell me. Did you find someone to buy the nugget?"

"Yes, I did."

"How do I find him? Where do I go?" White Feather's voice raced excitedly, her eyes dancing.

"You won't have to find him."

"What do you mean?"

"I have the money for you already."

White Feather could scarcely believe her ears. She was stunned. She knew Doc would help her but she didn't think that selling the gold piece would take place this soon or be this easy.

"What?" she asked unbelievingly.

"I have the money. It is a fair price for the nugget; in fact, more than it is actually worth," he said, drawing an envelope from the inside breast pocket of his coat. "Here you are," he said, handing the envelope to White Feather.

Her hands trembled when she took the envelope and she smiled. "Thank you, Doc. Thank you so much."

"Well, aren't you going to open it?" he teased.

"Yes," she laughed and tore open the envelope. The empty pouch with it's leather cord lay inside. But, then, her eyes widened at the amount of money.

"Doc...it is a lot of money," she gasped.

"Yes."

"It is too much, isn't it?"

"Not for the person who bought it. He wanted it very badly."

"How did you sell it so quickly? Who bought it?"

The old man smiled and shrugged his shoulders. "It is not important."

"But it is so much money; more than it is worth, I am sure. Please, tell me. Who bought it?"

"Let's just say that it was a friend who wants you to be happy."

"You are not going to tell me who bought it, are you?"

"No," he grinned.

White Feather fingered the bills and shook her head in disbelief, still surprised at the amount of money she received for the gold piece.

"Let me pay you now for the care you gave me after my attack," she said, holding bills out to the doctor.

"No, your bill has already been paid."

"Been paid?"

"Yes."

"By whom?"

Silence.

"Tell me, Doc," White Feather insisted. "Who did this? Tsu-la?"

"No."

"Who, then?"

"Michael."

"Michael?"

"Yes."

She put the money back in the envelope and quickly tucked it in her blouse when she heard Tsu-la's voice outside talking to Mrs. Shepherd. He had returned for her.

Looking deep into Doc's eyes she smiled at the kind man. "Doc, thank you. You are a good friend. I will always be grateful to you." She left the room, leaving the doctor staring after her.

A few minutes later he joined Mrs. Shepherd on the porch and the two of them watched while Tsu-la's wagon disappeared down the road.

"I've always dreamed of owning a gold nugget," the doctor said.

"Well, now your dream has come true," she grinned at the doctor.

"Yes," he said with a sigh, "but, I'll miss that girl...."

"I will too."

"...and Michael," the doctor added.

"Michael?" Mrs. Shepherd wondered what on earth the doctor meant.

CHAPTER FIFTY-TWO

I'll Miss You Forever

White Feather sat alone on the porch gently rocking, staring up at the star-sprinkled sky. Everyone else had gone to bed long ago. She was not sleepy despite the late evening hour. Excited, yet needing to think clearly, she had chosen the solitude. Two obstacles had appeared; two that had not occurred to her previously and she couldn't understand how she could have overlooked them.

She had been so preoccupied with selling the nugget that she had failed to make plans on how she would purchase the supplies without being noticed by someone who might tell Michael or Tsu-la. And where would she store the supplies until she was ready to leave?

She sat for a long time pondering every possibility but had found no solution. Now it appeared that there was no alternative except to tell her plans to Tsu-la and Marie...and Michael. He would have to be told too. How she dreaded facing them with the news of her leaving, but it seemed the only thing she could do. She had no place to hide the supplies even if she purchased them unnoticed. Tsu-la owned the largest store in town and carried most of the supplies she would need.

"Horses!" she thought suddenly. She would need two horses – one for herself and one for the children. They would need them for at least part of the trip. She would have to buy the horses and begin teaching the children to ride immediately. She knew that Tsu-la would question her about why she had been able to purchase them so she might as well tell everyone about her plans to leave. It was the only way.

She sighed deeply and folded her arms across the front of her body, leaned her head back and closed her eyes in resignation. She would tell her friends tomorrow. To delay telling them would only be delaying her trip. She would buy the horses in the morning.

Suddenly she heard the sound of approaching hoof beats on the road. She sat up straight and listened more closely. Who would be coming to Tsu-la's house this late in the evening? She stood and walked to the edge of the porch and strained her eyes to try to see the approaching rider but the night was too dark to see very far down the road. Should she call Tsu-la? No. She would wait until the horse came closer so she could see the rider more clearly. She stood quietly waiting, puzzled at the unusualness of such a late caller. She feared that something must be wrong.

The rider came nearer; she could see the person slouched over in the saddle, head bent. But she could not determine the identity of the rider. She turned to go inside to wake Tsu-la when the rider straightened himself wearily in the saddle and looked toward the house.

"Michael?" White Feather said softly.

No answer.

"Michael, is that you?" she called.

The horse and rider were nearer now and she could see that the rider was indeed Michael and she hurried down the steps to meet him.

He slowed the horse to a stop and looked at

White Feather but did not speak.

"Michael, what is wrong? Why have you come here so late in the evening?"

Michael slowly dismounted, not answering White Feather. Instead he put his arm around her and guided her back to the porch and into a chair then sat in the chair beside her. His haggard eyes peered at her.

"White Feather, I received bad news tonight."

"What has happened, Michael?"

"My mother is dead."

White Feather leaned toward Michael and put both of her arms around him and pulled him close to her.

"I am so sorry."

"She died in her sleep, peacefully," he said over the lump in his throat.

White Feather hugged him tighter and whispered, "Let me wake Tsu-la. He will want to know."

"All right" Michael said, gently pulling away from White Feather.

She arose, patted Michael tenderly on the shoulder and went into the house.

Moments later she returned followed by Tsu-la.

One friend clasped the other's hand. "Please accept my sympathy, Michael. Is there anything I can do for you?" he asked.

Michael's head slowly moved from side to side.

"What can I do for you, Michael?" he repeated. "Please, let me help. Tell me of your plans."

"I will need to go to Augusta as soon as possible. There is much to do in the family business. I will have to attend to the selling of mother's house, disposing of things," his voice broke emotionally. "Since my father passed away a few years back, it's all up to me."

"I understand, my friend. You do not need to talk of it now," Tsu-la said caringly.

"Thank you."

"What can we do for you here while you are gone?"

"I would be grateful if you would look in on my

business from time to time to see if things are going smoothly."

"Yes, of course."

"I have good men working for me who can manage well when I am not around but go by when you can to see if they need anything."

"Yes."

"Thank you."

"Michael, when are you leaving?"

"Tomorrow."

White Feather placed her hand on Michael's arm and looked up into his face. "Tomorrow? You are leaving tomorrow?"

"Yes. I will need to leave early tomorrow morning," he answered.

"When will you return?" she asked.

"I don't know. Three or four weeks probably. It's hard to say."

White Feather walked to the edge of the porch. She did not want Michael to see the tears forming in her eyes. She could not tell him she was leaving. She could not add more heartache for him, not now.

"White Feather," Michael said, following her.

Tsu-la put his hand on Michael's shoulder and broke in. "Michael, I will come to town very early in the morning to help you with your departure. I will see you then," he said, feeling that Michael and White Feather needed to be alone.

"Thank you, Tsu-la."

After Tsu-la went into the house Michael took White Feather into his arms and held her close.

"Come with me, White Feather," he whispered softly.

"What?"

"Come with me to Augusta."

"No, I cannot."

"I know," he said, thinking she refused because she would not leave the children. "But I do not want to leave you, even for a few weeks."

He pulled her closer to him and felt the wet tears on her face.

"Oh, White Feather, don't cry," he said, wiping the wetness from her cheeks, "please, don't cry."

"I'm sorry. I didn't mean to...."

"It's all right."

"I'm sorry about your mother."

He did not respond.

"I'm going to miss you so much," she whispered, realizing that she would never see Michael again after tonight.

"I'll miss you, too. I promise I will be back sooner than you can imagine. I won't be gone longer than a month, I am sure. I will come back as soon as I can, I promise." He managed a smile as he placed his fingertips under her chin and tilted her face upward so he could kiss her tenderly. "I love you, White Feather," he said. In his emotional state, he did not notice her lack of response. "I must go now. I have much to do to get ready to leave."

"Yes, I know."

He released her and started down the steps, paused, and turned. He took her into his arms and kissed her passionately this time. Then, he quickly left while White Feather stood on the porch watching him through a veil of tears.

"I will miss you forever, my dearest Michael. You will always remain in my heart," she whispered as she watched him walk out of her life.

CHAPTER FIFTY-THREE

A Different Kind of Love

The night after Michael left, when the children had been put to bed, she told Tsu-la and Marie of her plans.

The three of them were sitting on the porch enjoying the warm night when White Feather began. She told them about the nugget Running Deer had given her and her promise to him before he died.

"So, I am going home soon," she concluded.

"But White Feather, we thought that you were happy here with us," Marie said, shocked and saddened by her friend's words.

"I will always be indebted to you and Tsu-la, Marie. You have been good to me and cared for the children. I thank you for this. I love you both...and your children. But I have to go home."

Marie began to cry softly. "We will miss you so much, White Feather," she said. Then she got up and hugged White Feather and went into the house.

Tsu-la, surprised at White Feather's sudden declaration, said nothing, deep in thought about her decision to leave.

The two friends sat in silence for a long time.

Finally Tsu-la spoke.

"White Feather, you cannot take two small children and travel all the way back to Cherokee lands by yourself."

White Feather reached out and put her hand to Tsu-la's shoulder and looked into his face. "I have to go, Tsu-la. Please try to understand...please," she begged.

He nodded his head in agreement, "Yes, I understand. I suppose I always knew that you would go back one day."

During the following day Tsu-la was very helpful in planning the route. He chose two of the best horses from Michael's livery stable that White Feather insisted on paying for. He taught the children how to ride in the weeks before White Feather was ready to leave. She spent her last day by going into town to bid farewell to Doc, Mrs. Shepherd and Sa-lo-li. There had been sadness, but happy wishes intertwined.

"White Feather, we have not spoken about this since we found out that you were leaving, but what about Michael?" Marie had asked timidly, searching White Feather's face for an answer. "Do you love him? Really love him?"

"Yes, I love him, Marie, and I want to be with him, but I have to go home...and the weather is getting colder."

"Does he know you're leaving?"

"No," White Feather responded quietly. "I could not tell him."

"Why, White Feather?" Marie questioned, laying her hand on her friend's arm.

"Michael is happy here, Marie. He has his new house, his business."

Marie interrupted. "But he will not have you."

"I know." White Feather looked out into the distance then spoke again. "Someday he will find someone else to love." She hesitated, then continued, "Marie, I just have to go back. The mountains are my home, the love that fills my soul."

"More than Michael?"

White Feather dropped her head and for a moment did not answer. Then her words crawled out. "It's a different kind of love."

"If you knew you were going back east, White Feather, why didn't you ask Michael to go with you?"

"I don't know...." White Feather shook her head.

"He loves the mountains, you know. I've heard him talk about their beauty. He would be happy there, White Feather."

The longing in White Feather's heart filled her eyes. "Please tell him I thought it would be easier for me to leave while he's gone."

"You should have told him, White Feather," Marie said gently.

"I know. I feel badly about that," she responded.

"Why don't you wait to leave until he returns?" Marie insisted. "He should return soon."

"No. He will try to persuade me to stay and I cannot. Besides, it is time to go. The nearing cold weather will not wait for his return."

Marie shook her head, knowing that her words would not change White Feather's decision. She took her friend's hand and the women stood up facing each other.

"We will miss you and the children."

"And we will miss all of you. Thank you both for your kindness and all that you have done for us. I am truly grateful," she said, nodding to Tsu-la, who had come outside and was standing nearby on the porch.

White Feather saw that his eyes were moist but he managed a brief smile. "We will miss you, White Feather," he said.

The young women hugged briefly then stepped away from each other.

White Feather went into Tsu-la's open arms, clinging to him. When he released her she brushed away the tears on her face and smiled at them.

"Tsu-la has promised that we will visit you in the east sometime, White Feather," said Marie.

"I would like that. I will look forward to that day," she said, then added brightly, "Please make it soon."

The next morning before sunrise White Feather and her children left the house quietly, slipping noiselessly into the darkness to begin their long journey. White Feather sat tall on her horse, smiling, while she rode further and further down the road. The day she had eagerly anticipated for so long had finally arrived. She was going home...home to the mountains.

As they silently rode away from the house, Tsula stood at a window in the dark house watching until they were out of sight. Part of his heart longed to ride beside them.

CHAPTER FIFTY-FOUR

The Letter

Michael's love for White Feather deepened even more during their separation. He was anxious to get home. She had never been out of his thoughts and he couldn't wait to tell her about the surprising discovery he had made while going through his mother's old trunk of keepsakes. He hoped his news would please her.

It had been necessary for Michael to remain in Augusta for over a month. He had not anticipated that settling his mother's affairs would require so much more time than he had expected, but he had finally completed his business and would soon be on his way back to the west.

Michael had arrived in Augusta after his mother's funeral; in his absence his mother's sister, who also resided in Augusta, had taken care of the arrangements for the service and burial.

It took no time to sell his mother's home; it would take longer to decide what to keep from her belongings...and how to forget the memories that flooded his mind. Opening the old trunk in his mother's bedroom would complete the job, but he had stalled. He was certain that his mother had filled it to capacity through the years, and the emotion of touching the contents was almost more than he could handle. The last hand to caress the old photographs and keepsakes had been hers...even her scent lingered.

He sighed and began. By the time he had emptied the trunk of about half of its contents, a large envelope bearing his name caught his eye. He pulled it from under a stack of papers and read the message on the front written in his mother's beautiful handwriting: *"To Michael - From Your Mother."*

He ripped open the envelope. Inside he found a letter from his mother and a smaller sealed envelope. The letter read:

"Dear Michael,

I have enclosed a document that might surprise and even shock you. In 1833, the last of the Cherokee Indian lands in Georgia were entered in a land lottery held in our state capital in Milledgeville. There had been previous lotteries for the Georgia land but your father had shown no interest in them; however, when the last lottery was held he was persuaded by a friend to participate. Included in the lottery, 160 lots of farmland and 40 acres of gold mining sites were offered. Your father and his friend attended. Your father was not interested in the gold sites, but to humor his friend, he registered for the drawing of the farmland, never expecting to win. 85,000 people competed for the land sites and much to your father's surprise, his name was drawn as a winner of one of the 160 lots. He paid the $18.00 grant fee and returned home with the land deed. Winners were forbidden by the state to occupy their lots if any of the Cherokee people lived on them, but your father became curious about his property so before he became ill, he searched and found his land. He arrived near dusk that day and he told me how he stood, unobserved in the edge of the woods joining his property and saw a small log cabin sitting on a rise near the river. He saw a young Cherokee couple sitting on the porch. *"They looked so happy," your father told me when he returned home. "Not wishing to disturb them I quietly slipped away unnoticed and came back to Augusta."*

Michael, your father was never proud of the fact that he had participated in the land lottery. We both felt that it was wrong and inhuman to exile the Indians from their lands and he never returned to his lottery land – even after the removal was over.

I know how you felt about the removal also. Perhaps you may not want the land deed. You might choose to sell the land. It is yours now. Use it in whatever way you desire. It is your property.

Lovingly,

Your Mother"

Michael was stunned. His hands trembled as he reread the letter and then read it yet again.

Finally he opened the smaller envelope containing the deed and stared at it. Attached was a map of the land plot drawn in the lottery. He took a pen from his pocket and carefully circled his plot of land on the map.

From his military duty in the Indian Territory he had become familiar with the Cherokee lands and he knew the approximate location of the lot. The memory burned in his mind...he would never forget the beauty. He had known about the lottery when it had occurred and remembered that some of the lottery winners did not wait to claim their land, forcing the Cherokee occupying the sites to leave their property. He recalled the greed of some of the white people to take the Cherokee lands and it had sickened him.

Now he was a lottery-land owner. What should he do with the land?

He would ask White Feather.

CHAPTER FIFTY-FIVE

Home Again

It was a late September afternoon. White Feather sat wearily on her horse. She glanced at the children riding together following closely behind her.

"We will soon be home," she said softly over her shoulder, "back where we belong."

Her children had been well behaved on the journey mapped out by Tsu-la, but she knew that they were tired. At times she had seen them dozing on their horse while riding, or nibbling on the jerky Marie had sent with them. Nodding in exhaustion, neither one of them had complained or cried during the entire trip.

Unlike her children, White Feather had shed many tears when no one could see her. Every time she thought of Michael, her eyes swam. She missed him and desperately wanted to be with him. During the first few days of the trip she had almost turned around several times to go back to Tsu-la's house to wait for Michael.

She knew now that she truly loved him and this knowledge surprised her for she thought she could never love another man after she lost Running Deer.

But then, all thoughts of Michael vanished. The mountains...her mountains...were there before her. White Feather's body quivered with excitement. The feeling had started when she began seeing the gentle rolling hills in the distance. She could see the faint blue-green mountain tops coming into view and the anticipation of nearing her homeland had been almost overwhelming to her during the past two hours.

She dug her heels gently into her horse's sides, prodding him to move faster. She could hardly wait to get home. The huge mountains were beginning to appear closer in front of her and she smiled at them, almost laughing aloud from sheer joy.

"This is where I am supposed to be," she whispered softly, looking at the tall peaks. "I belong here."

She neared the road leading to the village where Cherokee friends lived before the removal and wondered who was living there now, but she refused to delay the return to her homesite any longer.

"I will go there later," she thought, turning her horse away.

The narrow path was covered over with leaves and undergrowth from the lack of use, but even after an absence of over two years, White Feather had no difficulty following the familiar trail.

Waves of anticipation washed over her. Her hands trembled from the excitement she felt pulsing through her body. She was home!

"The forest is beautiful. Soon I will be at my cabin," she said anxiously. Suddenly her thoughts halted. "My cabin?" she said, pulling up on the reins, slowing the horse. "It is not there anymore," she whispered, remembering the fire and the horrible black smoke boiling from the cabin while the soldiers pushed her down the path away from her home.

The sun's rays sliced their light between the trees casting shadows on the forest floor and White Feather looked into the woods with watery eyes, trying to dismiss the memory of the terrible day when they left to walk to the west.

"I am back now," she thought brightly. "The land is still here. The beautiful trees, the sparkling river, the mountains."

"This is where we lived, Gv-nv-ge Yo-na and Little Fawn. Isn't it beautiful here?" she said.

The sound of water rushing over rocks slipped into the quietness of the woods and White Feather straightened her body, raising herself to look in the direction of the familiar sound and strained her eyes.

"The river. We are near the river," she said happily. She snapped the reins and encouraged the horse to move at a faster pace. She turned toward the children and cast a smile in their direction.

"Little Fawn...Gv-nv-ge Yo-na! Do you hear the river?"

The children listened and eagerly nodded catching the contagious delight of their mother.

"We will go to the water and swim," she promised her children.

They squealed in anticipation and laughed out loud with her.

When White Feather's horse rounded the bend on the trail she stopped abruptly, pulling up on the reins quickly. She gasped, then caught her breath and began breathing in short, quick pants.

"Stop!" she whispered to the children, motioning with her hand.

Her heart beat rapidly and her breath remained ragged as she sat motionless, staring.

Standing alone in the middle of the clearing was the tall stone chimney, the lone surviving part of what was once her cabin home, looming directly in front of her. It stood like a sentinel guarding this place, waiting for her return.

Sadness flooded her body and she fought back the tears forming in her eyes. She had not expected that seeing the cabin site again would affect her heart so deeply. The stone chimney was all that remained of the cabin, except for the debris scattered about on the ground and a few rocks that had once been the steps of the cabin.

"This is where we lived," she told her children softly. "The cabin is gone now but it was beautiful."

She sat for a moment staring at the stone structure.

"We were happy here," she added over the lump in her throat.

Slowly she slid from her horse and walked toward the rise in the land where her cabin had once stood.

"Come," she motioned for the children to follow.

She walked past the split rail fence, still standing, but now overgrown with weeds and grass. Her eyes followed the fence and she thought of Running Deer. He had worked many days splitting the rails and then carefully forming the fence around the cabin and the barn. The barn. She looked in the direction where it had stood. It was gone too. Burned to the ground.

She glanced around the clearing and saw no one. She was surprised that the land had not been occupied. She had heard about the lottery in Georgia before she left on the western march.

She approached the tall chimney and stood looking up at it. White Feather put out her hand and caressed one of the large rocks.

"Your father built this chimney by himself," she told Little Fawn and Gv-nv-ge Yo-na. She rubbed her hand across the rocks remembering the handsome young Indian man, bare to the waist, his rippling muscles bulging in his back and arms each time he lifted a stone to put it in place to form the chimney.

"Each rock was carefully selected by him on every trip he made down to the river to gather them," she said. "He was very proud of the chimney,"

White Feather's eyes clouded over. Her love for Running Deer remained, never to leave her heart.

"I came back, Running Deer, just as I promised you," she said softly, her gaze now directed to the soft blue sky. "Our children will grow up in the land of our people. We will find a place to live and we will never leave our homeland again."

"Swim! Go swim!" Gv-nv-ge Yo-na's voice impatiently interrupted his mother's thoughts.

White Feather turned and looked at her son who looked so much like his father.

She smiled. "Come. We will all go to the water."

CHAPTER FIFTY-SIX

The Stone Chimney

Michael held the lottery land map in his hand, his eyes gazing intently at the land plots while he rode slowly along the river's edge. He had become curious about his newly acquired property and had decided to locate the site on his trip back to the west. He pulled up on the horse's reins and stopped, wiped the perspiration from his brow and squinted at the map again. He was weary and anxious to get back home to see White Feather and he had almost halted his search yesterday.

He had been searching for days and finally, with the help of a trading post owner at the last settlement he had passed, he had been directed toward the land. As well as he could determine from the map and the store owner's directions he was close to the site now. At times the countryside had seemed vaguely familiar to him but he wasn't sure. He had followed the river, riding at its edge, because he knew that his land bordered the bank and would be easier to locate from that direction.

His head bowed low studying the map, he prodded the horse. He knew that he had to be close to his destination according to the map. He looked up and blinked his tired eyes several times. The land looked extremely familiar now. He halted the horse again and looked away from the river toward a rise in the clearing. He squinted and saw something on top of the rise...a stone chimney. Yes, this was the place, he had finally arrived. According to the storekeeper his lot had an old rock chimney standing on it.

He leaned forward in his saddle, wiped the back of his hand over his eyes and looked again.

"Is that someone standing by the chimney?" he thought. "Two horses? Are my eyes deceiving me?"

He rubbed his eyes and looked toward the rise once again.

"There are two children sitting on one of the horses," he thought.

He had seen no one all day. Was he imagining this?

He began riding slowly away from the river toward the chimney. His horse shook its head and snorted loudly.

Little Fawn and Gv-nv-ge Yo-na heard the noise and turned to look at the approaching horse and rider. Little Fawn recognized Michael immediately and screamed in excitement. She jumped off her horse and started running toward him.

White Feather turned just as Gv-nv-ge Yo-na slid from the horse and began sprinting behind Little Fawn. The children were shouting Michael's name as they ran toward him.

He leaped from his horse laughing and running toward the children with his arms outstretched.

White Feather put her hand over her eyes to shade them from the sun and stood looking at the man and the children.

"Michael?" she whispered in disbelief. "It's not possible!"

Little Fawn and Gv-nv-ge Yo-na reached Michael and he stooped down and swooped both of them into his arms. The force of their excitement almost knocked him to the ground. They clung to him in a tangle of arms and legs, hugging him as if they would never let him go.

White Feather stood frozen in shock. Her knees began trembling, threatening to buckle under her.

"Is it really Michael?"

He put the children down, took each one by the hand, and began walking toward White Feather. He wore a broad smile on his face.

"Michael," she whispered, moving slowly toward him, then after a few steps she quickened her pace.

Michael dropped the children's hands and sped toward White Feather.

"I thought I would never see you again!" she said running into his arms. "I thought I had lost you forever!"

"Never! White Feather, you will never lose me."

White Feather lost herself in the wonder of the moment.

Nearby the children stood giggling at the scene taking place between their mother and Michael.

"The children and I came home," White Feather pulled herself from the man's arms to explain.

"Yes," he said, smiling at her. "We are home now. We never have to leave here again."

"But your home is in the west, Michael."

"My home is where you are, White Feather."

"The cabin...it is gone."

"We will build another; right here by the river."

"But the land is still...."

"It is your land now," he said, drawing the land deed from his shirt pocket and waving it in her face."Well...it's ours," he nodded, "from the land lottery." He began to walk around the area, throwing out his arms and smiling.

She returned his smile; then, suddenly gasped. "But Michael." she cried, "I left you to return home."

Michael interrupted. "It doesn't matter, White Feather; for even the universe seems to want us together...'cause here I am, too. It's no coincidence."

He had stopped at the chimney and stood looking up

at it. He leaned into the structure and placed both hands upon its stones.

"Look, White Feather," he called, "Looks like this chimney...this spirit of fire...is still standing guard."

Beyond Michael, beyond the chimney's rounded stones, White Feather could see the blue-gray mist of the mountains. Her fingers felt for the leather cord that still hung about her neck. She touched it's empty pouch. Gazing at the shape of the man caught within the shadow of the mist of the mountains, from somewhere deep within herself, a new fire kindled and she felt the power as the souls of her two loves connected.

"Gv-ge-yu...I love you," she whispered as a sudden warm gust of autumn wind pushed her skirt against her legs. "Michael of my heart...we are home."

Epilogue

Cherokee Today

Today there are over 12,000 enrolled members of the Eastern Band of Cherokee Indians. With the exception of around 400 members, the Indians live on 56,000 acres of land in the small corner of Western North Carolina known as the Qualla Boundary or the Cherokee Indian Reservation.

Approximately 17,000 Cherokee began the walk to the Indian Territory in the west. More than 5,000—nearly one third of the Cherokee population—died along the way. The walk later became known as the Trail of Tears.

Like White Feather, many ancestors of those who walked the Trail of Tears made their way back home after the exile was completed. A small number of Cherokee who hid in the mountains to evade capture survived. It is their descendants who make up the larger population on the reservation today.

When I began this book, I knew I had to learn much more about the Cherokee people and their lives. I spent many hours researching the events told in this story. Being an associate member of the Museum of the Cherokee Indian, I visited the Archives Department each time I had a question or needed information. As an employee of the Cherokee Historical Association, I used this opportunity to also gather information, to talk to the Cherokee actors as they prepared to perform in *Unto These Hills*, to learn about their feelings and hopes for the future.

I spent time with the craftspeople of the Oconaluftee Indian Village, learning more about the Cherokee's way of life during the time that White Feather lived. As I shaped my story, I allowed White Feather to stroll along the nature trail at the Village, to watch her people as they told of their culture, while their fingers wove baskets, turned pottery, did bead work. She drank in the very essence of her people.

My Cherokee friends Jerry, Bo, Jean, Ben, Emaline, Lucy and others were so very kind in answering the many pointed questions I had regarding the lifestyle and the thoughts of White Feather and Running Deer. I am indebted to them.

The children of Cherokee also added their flavor in my discussions with them as their substitute teacher, suggesting situations and filling in the solutions.

At one time I was not sure I would ever complete this book. My home burned and the flames took half of my manuscript. Then, in my despair, White Feather's piercing eyes again ignited the fire within me and my thoughts and fingers picked up the weave once more.

History and traditions of the Cherokee people are today continually perpetuated in the outdoor drama *Unto These Hills*, the Oconaluftee Indian Village and the Museum of the Cherokee Indian.

Cherokee are strong people. They cherish their land, their language, their arts, crafts and culture.

They are a proud race of people.

Their past is a story of survival.

Their present is a story of growth and successes.

Their future is a story of hope and determination.

Today, as I sit looking out the window at the beautiful mountains surrounding my home, I smile. This is Cherokee land; it belongs to the Cherokee again.

Remembering White Feather, the courageous young Cherokee woman, I believe her undying spirit will move forever among the tranquil hills and valleys of her beloved home. White Feather touched my heart.

I had to tell her story.

—Nancy McIntosh Pafford
2004

Other books by the author
*CHEROKEE ROSE
  (Second book in the
    WHITE FEATHER trilogy)
*JANIE OF CHEROKEE
  (Third book)
These can be ordered from the autho

About the Author

Nancy McIntosh Pafford

Nancy is a native of South Georgia and a retried school teacher. As a child she and her family traveled to Cherokee, NC on vacations where she attended the drama, *"Unto These Hills,"* each year. It was during these visits that her love for the mountains and its culture was born.

After she married and had a family of her own, she introduced her husband and two sons to the Smoky Mountains and they enjoyed many family vacations there.

Through the years her heart has always been drawn to the Cherokee people and their land. In time, she was inspired to tell their story through *White Feather.*

Nancy retired and moved to Cherokee after she became a widow and one son, Bryan, was killed while serving in the armed forces. Her other son, Tim, resides in South Georgia.

Nancy always dreamed of living in Cherokee and teaching the Cherokee children. Now, her dream has come true. She enjoys substitute teaching and working part time with the Cherokee Historical Association. She attends Cherokee United Methodist Church where she serves as the church pianist and is dedicated to the young people and elders alike. She is also an assoicate member of the Museum of the Cherokee Indian in Cherokee.

Through these experiences she has gained much insight into the culture of the Cherokee, which has nurtured her own Native American family background. Although she is not an enrolled member of the tribe, her dedication to the Cherokee people is evident within the words of her novel, *White Feather.*

For additional copies of this book, please complete on a separate sheet of paper the following details:

Name _____

Address _____

_____

Phone (in case of returns) _____

_____ books @ $15.95 = _____

Tax @ GA 7%=   _____
(Tax due from Georgia residents only)

Shipping and Handling
$3.50 per book   _____

Total of order   _____

Send to the following address:

Nancy M. Pafford
P.O. Box 528
Lakeland, Georgia 31635

❑ I am interested in receiving more information about how to acquire Nancy Pafford as a speaker for our club or civic meeting, dinner meeting, book club, a book signing...or _____.

216